The Ha

Richa

methuen | drama

LONDON · NEW YORK · OXFORD · NEW DELHI · SYDNEY

METHUEN DRAMA
Bloomsbury Publishing Plc
50 Bedford Square, London, WC1B 3DP, UK
1385 Broadway, New York, NY 10018, USA
29 Earlsfort Terrace, Dublin 2, Ireland

BLOOMSBURY, METHUEN DRAMA and the Methuen
Drama logo are trademarks of Bloomsbury Publishing Plc

First published in Great Britain 2024

Copyright © Richard Molloy, 2024

Richard Molloy has asserted his right under the Copyright, Designs
and Patents Act, 1988, to be identified as author of this work.

Cover image © Charles Deluvio/ Unsplash

All rights reserved. No part of this publication may be reproduced or
transmitted in any form or by any means, electronic or mechanical, including
photocopying, recording, or any information storage or retrieval system,
without prior permission in writing from the publishers.

Bloomsbury Publishing Plc does not have any control over, or responsibility
for, any third-party websites referred to or in this book. All internet addresses
given in this book were correct at the time of going to press. The author and
publisher regret any inconvenience caused if addresses have changed or sites
have ceased to exist, but can accept no responsibility for any such changes.

No rights in incidental music or songs contained in the work are hereby
granted and performance rights for any performance/presentation
whatsoever must be obtained from the respective copyright owners.

All rights whatsoever in this play are strictly reserved and application
for performance etc. should be made before rehearsals to The Theseus
Agency, 29 Rosslyn Hill, London NW3 5UJ (email: info@theseus.agency).
No performance may be given unless a licence has been obtained.

A catalogue record for this book is available from the British Library.

A catalog record for this book is available from the Library of Congress.

ISBN: PB: 978-1-3505-0438-7
ePDF: 978-1-3505-0439-4
eBook: 978-1-3505-0440-0

Series: Modern Plays

Typeset by Mark Heslington Ltd, Scarborough, North Yorkshire
Printed and bound in Great Britain

To find out more about our authors and books visit
www.bloomsbury.com and sign up for our newsletters.

The Harmony Test was first performed at Hampstead Theatre Downstairs, London, on 17 May 2024. The cast was as follows:

Zoe	**Pearl Chanda**
Kash	**Bally Gill**
Naomi	**Jemima Rooper**
Rocco	**Sandro Rosta**
Charlie	**Milo Twomey**

Writer	Richard Molloy

Director	Alice Hamilton
Designer	Sarah Beaton
Lighting	Jamie Platt
Sound	Harry Blake
Costume Supervisor	Molly Syrett
Fight Director	Bret Yount
Stage Manager	Jack Sheffield
Assistant Stage Manager	Chloe Forestier-Walker

Thank you

Greg Ripley-Duggan, Katharine Noble, Lauren King, Rhianna Biggs, Lucie Blockley, Davina Moss, Roxana Silbert, Celia Atkin, Clare Jepson-Homer, Pascale Giudicelli, Sarah Beaton, Jamie Platt, Harry Blake, Bret Yount, Molly Syrett, Jack Sheffield, Chloe Forestier-Walker, Bally Gill, Pearl Chanda, Jemima Rooper, Milo Twomey, Sandro Rosta, Shane Zaza, Esther Smith, Daniel Fraser, Akshay Sharan, Jon Foster, Lily Nichol, Moe Bar-El, Louise Ripley-Duggan, Colette O'Dwyer, Neil Darby, Philip Molloy, Sheila Wayman, Bryan and Anne Andrews, and Frank and Patricia Byrne.

Special thanks to Alice Hamilton, Susan Stanley, Mary Meyler, and Laura Molloy.

The Harmony Test

For Laura, Riley and Annie

Characters

Zoe, *thirties*
Kash, *thirties*
Naomi, *forties*
Charlie, *forties*
Rocco, *twenties*

Setting

A kitchen in a rented apartment in present-day London.

Notes

Kash is a secular Muslim. The rest of the casting should reflect the diversity of contemporary London.

An ellipsis (. . .) after a character's name indicates an unwillingness or an inability to speak.

A forward slash (/) indicates where the next line of dialogue begins.

Act One

Scene One

Mid-morning.

A kitchen in a run-down two-bedroom flat on the ground floor of a once rather grand Edwardian property, now converted into over-priced apartments. With a distant, indifferent landlord, the kitchen, though clean and tidy, is in a state of borderline disrepair: cheap, aging IKEA furniture and kitchenware; broken fittings; peeling paint; traces of mould in the corners of the windows. A dining table with mismatched chairs. A rickety bookshelf. A wedding photograph. Some house plants. A wifi speaker. Box files containing bills and other paperwork.

Two doors: one leads to a hallway and the rest of the flat; the other, the rear entrance to the property, gives access to a back passageway, outdoor bins, etc.

At lights up, **Zoe** *and* **Kash** *are sitting at the kitchen table.* **Zoe** *has an iPad (or similar device) and a notebook and pen. She is showing* **Kash** *something on the iPad.*

Zoe   Okay, so, it's pretty straightforward really. What it does – It calculates for you – based on the length of your cycle, the timing of your last period, that sorta thing – It figures out which days of the month you're more likely to conceive . . .

Kash (*not understanding the implication*)   . . . Right . . .?

Zoe   . . . And those are the days you . . .

Kash   . . . Oh! Oh, I see! That's when we . . .

Zoe   Yes –

Kash (*stadium announcement*)   'Play ball!' So to speak.

Zoe   So to speak.

Kash   No, I'm with you now.

Zoe   Good –

Kash   So this – the app – It creates like a – like a timetable?

Zoe   Well, not exactly –

Kash   Friday the seventh at 8 p.m. –

Zoe   It's not that specific –

Kash (*mock clinical*)   Initiate coitus.

Zoe   Are you taking this seriously?

Kash   Yes, I am –

Zoe   Because, actually, what we call it – the language we use – it's important.

Kash   Of course –

Zoe   It's not a timetable.

Kash   Okay –

Zoe   It's a fertility plan.

Kash   Right. Sure. What's the difference?

Zoe   The difference is . . . There is a vast chasm of difference . . .

She can't articulate the difference.

. . . It doesn't fucking matter what the difference is –

Kash   No –

Zoe   What *does* matter – This thing tells us – with a high degree of accuracy – when we can –

Kash (*sex voice*)   Get it on –

Zoe   Become pregnant.

Kash   Precisely.

Zoe   So, for example, let's take a look at this month.

Kash   Great –

Zoe (*pointing at the iPad*)   So these dates here . . .

Kash   Yes –

Zoe   Conception is unlikely.

Kash (*sings in a southern American accent*)   'Ain't no water in the well –'

Zoe (*cutting him off, pointing again*)   Whereas *here* – See –

Kash   Uh-huh –

Zoe   This is the window of optimum fertility.

Kash   Oooh! Sexy –

Zoe   So during this time –

Kash   We *can* –

Zoe   We *need* to –

Kash (*sex voice*)   Take a trip to love town –

Zoe   Have sex.

Kash   Alright!

Zoe   Copious sex.

Beat.

Kash   Copious sex?

Zoe   Yes.

Kash   Meaning how much sex / exactly –?

Zoe   Once in the morning. Once at night.

Kash   Sex twice a day?

Zoe   Correct.

Kash   . . . Okay . . .

Zoe   Is that –?

Kash   That's fine.

Zoe   Are you sure?

Kash   Yep.

Zoe   It's not a problem?

Kash   Why would it be a problem?

Zoe   I dunno. I feel like there's some sorta – Like you're worried about something.

Kash   I'm not worried.

Zoe   Maybe you're anxious about having to perform so regularly –

Kash   Woah! Woah! Woah! Woah! Excuse me! *Excuse me!* I can perform regularly –

Zoe   You'll have plenty of time to recover in / between –

Kash   I don't need plenty of time to recover! I have zero problems in the recovery department!

Zoe   Okay. So . . .?

Kash   So nothing.

Zoe   . . . No issues? No concerns?

Kash   Absolutely none. 'Copious sex.' No complaints from me.

Zoe   Alright. Good. So, what I also wanted to / discuss –

Kash   I mean, twice a day is *a lot of sex* . . .

Zoe   It *is*, yes . . . Is it too much –?

Kash   No. No. Not at all –

Zoe   What then?

Kash   Nothing. No. It's just. Well. Okay. Sometimes. For a man. Too much action. You know, thrusting, pounding, that

sorta thing. Sometimes, it leads to . . . a . . . swelling. Of the
. . . penis.

Zoe   . . . A swelling of the penis?

Kash   Yes.

Zoe   . . . Isn't that a good thing?

Kash   I don't mean like an erection. That's – An erection is
an *upward* swelling, isn't it? This is more *outward*. Like a
puffy, misshapen, slightly grotesque . . . phenomenon. So,
the penis is swollen even when flaccid.

Zoe   Right.

Kash   You have – actually – You have seen it before.

Zoe   When?

Kash   When we – I don't know – Look, it's no big deal. All
I'm saying is maybe – *maybe* – once or twice during the sex
window –

Zoe   The window of optimum fertility –

Kash   During the – yeah – the thing – I may, possibly, need
to –

Zoe   You might need a / break –?

Kash   A night off.

Zoe   I see.

Kash   Is that . . .?

Zoe   I mean, it only lasts like six days –

Kash   No, I – I'm sure I can handle it – I'll be fine – I will.
I'm just saying – Just letting you know, *in case* . . .

Zoe   In case your penis –

Kash   In case it – yeah.

Zoe   Okay.

Kash   Okay.

Beat.

Zoe   But aside from that –

Kash   Aside from that –

Zoe   You're on board with the –?

Kash   I'm – yes – I'm fully on board with the timetable. (*Immediately corrects himself.*) The fertility plan, sorry –

Zoe   Alright. Excellent. Now. There are a couple of other things. I just wanna check in with you really.

Kash (*'go ahead'*)   Please.

Zoe   Have you been taking your supplements?

Kash   Yes.

Zoe   All of them?

Kash   All of the many, many supplements you so kindly purchased for me, yes.

Zoe   Every morning?

Kash   Every single morning.

Zoe   Good man. (*Ticking something off in her notebook.*) Supplements. Tick. And exercise?

Kash   Gym every day this week.

Zoe   Well done. Fabulous. (*Writing in her notebook again.*) That's another tick. And your diet?

Kash (*silly voice*)   Five a day, yo!

Zoe   Greens? Fruit? Whole grains? Proteins?

Kash (*silly voice*)   I'm all up in that shit!

Zoe (*makes another tick in her notebook*)   Wonderful. Wonderful. Alcohol?

Kash (*'Do you really need to ask?'*)   Zoe . . .

Zoe (*makes another note*)   No alcohol. Good. Ah. Now. What about the boxer shorts? How are they working out?

Kash   . . . Can I be honest?

Zoe   Yes.

Kash   I don't like 'em.

Zoe   Why not?

Kash   They're too loose.

Zoe   They're supposed to be loose. That's the whole point.

Kash   I know, but –

Zoe   We don't want your little scrotum overheating, do we, love?

Kash   No. Obviously. I get that. I'm just saying: I prefer wearing Y-fronts.

Zoe   I prefer having an intact vagina, but we agreed: I'll carry and birth the child. You wear the boxer shorts.

Kash   Sure. No problem.

Zoe   You promise?

Kash   I promise.

Zoe   Okay. Well then. (*Checking her notes.*) I think that's it for now.

Kash   Okay?

Zoe   Yep! We're all set!

Kash   Alright!

Zoe   Shall we get to it then?

Kash   . . . What, now? You wanna –?

Zoe   The window is open.

Kash *looks at the kitchen window before he realises –*

Kash   Oh, you mean the – right. Sorry –

Zoe (*sex voice*)   I'm feeling optimal.

Kash   Yeah, I understand – I've got an audition though. At like two.

Zoe   It's only half eleven.

Kash   You don't think we'll be long?

Zoe   It's not gonna take two and half hours, no.

Kash   No, right . . . Okay then. Alright. Let's –

Zoe   Good. Great. Just, eh, apply an ice pack to your testicles first, would you? For five minutes.

Kash   . . . What?

Zoe   Put some ice on your . . .

Kash   On my . . .?

Zoe   Your balls. Yes.

Kash   Why would I do that?

Zoe   To enhance the quality of your sperm, silly.

Kash   Oh. Right . . . Like a bag of peas – down –?

Zoe   Exactly.

Kash (*tentative*)   Okay.

Zoe   And when you're all done, I'll be waiting in the bedroom.

Kash   Sure . . .

Zoe   . . . Hey . . . I'm glad we're doing this together . . . I mean, I'm glad I'm doing it . . . with you.

Kash   Me too.

Zoe *exits.* **Kash** *goes to the freezer. He rummages around and removes a bag of frozen peas. For a moment, he considers how best to apply the bag to his testicles. He then pulls out the waistband of his trousers and eases the peas between his legs –*

Kash (*high-pitched*)   Oh, fuck me, that's cold!

Blackout.

Scene Two

Some months later.

Zoe *is tidying up after a meal.* **Kash** *is helping her.* **Naomi** *and* **Charlie** *are sitting at the table.*

Naomi   She's forgotten us.

Charlie   She hasn't forgotten us.

Naomi   She *has*. She hasn't even suggested coming home. Not once.

Charlie   It's only been two weeks. And it's far away. And the train tickets are expensive. Are you gonna pay for her to come home every weekend?

Naomi   It's nothing to do with the money. Or the distance. She's too busy *doing other things*. Shagging. And smoking crack.

Charlie   I sincerely doubt she's smoking crack.

Naomi   Are you saying she *is* shagging?

Charlie   It's possible.

Naomi   Oh my God –

Charlie   She's eighteen years old.

Naomi   She's my baby.

Charlie   No, she's not. Not anymore.

Naomi You don't even care. You don't even miss her.

Charlie Yes, I do. Absolutely, I do. I miss her. I'm just more – pragmatic about it. That's all. She's growing up. She's gone to uni. Which is great, actually. I wouldn't change it. We just need to accept it. Move on with the next phase of our lives.

Naomi There is no next phase of my life. I've served my function. My life is over.

Charlie Oh come on. You're not even fifty.

Naomi (*offended*) I'm forty-four.

Charlie Precisely. You've got loads of time.

Naomi Loads of time for what . . .? For eighteen years, my life was defined by my child. Now she's gone, what's left? Nothing.

Zoe You've still got your job, your friends –

Naomi I hate teaching, and you're the only friend I can tolerate.

Kash Maybe you need a hobby.

Charlie Right. Exactly. I told her to go to the gym.

Naomi Because I'm a fat bitch –

Charlie Because it would be good for you. Physically and psychologically.

Naomi I'm a fat, psychologically disturbed bitch.

Charlie I give up –

Naomi I'm not going to the gym. The gym is for narcissistic cunts.

Charlie Seriously –

Zoe Kash goes to the gym.

Naomi Narcissistic cunts – and actors.

Kash   There's a distinction, people!

Naomi   I was thinking about a dog.

Charlie   Please no. Not this.

Naomi   Yes, *this* –

Zoe   You wanna get a dog?

Naomi   Well, yeah –

Zoe   I think that's a great idea.

Kash   I love dogs.

Naomi   So do I.

Kash   Can *we* get a dog?

Zoe   Shush –

Charlie   We're not getting a dog.

Zoe   Why not?

Charlie   Not happening –

Naomi   You got something. You got a cake shop. I want a dog.

Charlie   How many times? It's not a cake shop. It is a *tea room*. And I didn't *get* it. Santa Claus didn't deliver it on his sleigh. It's not a toy. It's a massive financial and emotional commitment.

Naomi   I wanna make a massive financial and emotional commitment *to a dog*.

Kash   How is the cake shop? (*Corrects himself.*) Tea room, sorry. How's it going?

Charlie   Good, yeah. A lot of work.

Naomi   He spends all his time there.

Charlie   That's not true –

Naomi   So he never has to spend any with me.

Charlie   That is a lie –

Zoe   What's your objection to a dog, Charlie?

Naomi   He *claims* he's allergic.

Charlie   It's not a claim. It's a medical fact.

Naomi   A medical fact you neglected to mention for nineteen years. Until, coincidentally, I wanted a dog.

Charlie   I didn't mention it for nineteen years, because I didn't *need* to mention it, because you didn't wanna get a dog –

Zoe   How are you allergic?

Naomi   Oh yes, tell us how. With what terrible symptoms are you afflicted if you come into contact with a canine?

Charlie   I get puffy, swollen eyes. A runny nose. Itching. Potentially, worst-case scenario: anaphylactic shock. I die.

Naomi   / Fuck off.

Zoe   Really?

Charlie   It's true –

Naomi   Bullshit. I'm getting a dog. I've decided.

Charlie   *You*'ve decided?

Naomi   Yes.

Charlie   You can't make that decision on your own –

Naomi   I just did. My daughter's gone. I / need a replacement –

Charlie   She's not gone –

Naomi   / I need to love something –

Charlie   She's not dead. She's at university –

Naomi   I'm getting a dog –

Charlie   What about me? You can love me.

Naomi   Get serious, would you?

Charlie   I *am* serious.

Naomi   I can't love you.

Charlie   Why not?

Naomi   Look at you.

Charlie   What's wrong with me?

Naomi   . . . You're my husband. I can't love you.

Charlie   What –?

Zoe   That's a silly thing to say.

Naomi (*to* **Zoe**, *re* **Kash**)   Do you love him?

Zoe   . . . Huh?

Naomi   Do you love him?

Zoe   . . . Eh, yes.

Naomi   See! And they've only been married five minutes –

Charlie   She said yes!

Kash   She said yes –

Naomi   It wasn't a real yes! She hesitated –

Zoe   Of course, it was a real yes –

Kash   She didn't hesitate –

Zoe   I love him –

Charlie   Strange as it may sound, Naomi, it is possible for a woman to love her husband –

Naomi   No, no, no. You don't get it. I wanna *really love* something. I wanna *mother* something.

Charlie   Hold on. You want another baby? Is that what you're saying?

Naomi   Yes. Now you're talking.

Charlie   You've got to be fucking kidding me.

Naomi   What?

Charlie   I can't even – How often did I ask – How often did I *beg* / you to –?

Naomi   I'm allowed to change my mind.

Charlie   It's a bit bloody late for that, isn't it?

Naomi   Is it?

Charlie   Yes.

Naomi   Why?

Charlie   We're too old. Obviously.

Naomi   I'm not too old. My oven still works.

Charlie   You don't even want another baby. Not really –

Naomi   How would you know what I want?

Charlie   You've told me. A million times.

Naomi   Like I just said: I can change my mind –

Charlie   You haven't changed your mind though, have you? You hate babies.

Naomi   I do not!

Charlie   'Toddlers are cunts!' That's what you used to say.

Naomi   Toddlers *are* cunts. And teenagers too. But babies –

Charlie   No. I'm not having it. You hate babies an' all. You were miserable when Jada was born.

Naomi   What're you talking about?

Charlie   Maternity leave. Hello! You were depressed!

Naomi   I was not depressed!

Charlie   Okay. No, you weren't. I must've been living in an alternate reality.

Naomi   Well, now that you mention it: most of the time you weren't even there.

Charlie   What?! Of course I was there!

Naomi   No, you were not. You were at work. All day –

Charlie   / Oh here we go –

Naomi   – every day. As usual –

Charlie   Look. You know what. Fine. Let's have a baby then. Let's do it. Honestly, I would love to have another child . . . I'm serious. If you're up for it, so am I . . .

Naomi   . . . I don't actually think I want a baby. I was just making a point –

Charlie   Ah fuck off –

Kash   Maybe we should change the subject –

Naomi   I *am* getting a dog though.

Charlie   No, you're not.

Naomi   Yes, I am.

Charlie   *No, you're not.*

Naomi   You can't stop me –

Charlie (*loses his temper*)   Alright, Naomi! Enough now! Okay! Enough!

Naomi   . . . Alright. Calm down. Jeez.

Beat.

Kash (*clears his throat*)   . . . So, eh . . . Anyone see the Arsenal game / last night –?

Charlie   What about you two?

Kash   . . . What about us?

Charlie   When are you having a baby?

Zoe   . . .

Kash   . . .

Naomi   Are you a fucking moron?

Charlie   What? What have I done now?

Naomi   You can't ask that question.

Charlie   Can't I?

Naomi   No!

Charlie   Why not?

Naomi   Because. It's private.

Charlie   Okay . . . Sorry. I was only making conversation –

Naomi   Jesus Christ –

Charlie   Sorry. I'm sorry.

A moment of awkwardness before –

Zoe   Anyone for dessert?

Blackout.

Scene Three

Some months later.

Zoe *sits alone at the kitchen table, looking at her phone. Offstage, the main door of the flat opens and shuts. Shortly afterwards,* **Kash** *enters the kitchen.*

Kash (*concerned*)   Hey, how you feeling?

Zoe (*glum*)   Fine.

Kash   Come here.

Kash *gives* **Zoe** *a hug.*

Kash   When did you eh . . .?

Zoe   This morning. Right after you left.

Kash   Fuck. Sorry . . . I dunno what to say . . .

Zoe *shrugs.*

Kash   We'll keep trying, okay. We will.

Zoe   Mm-hmm.

Beat.

Kash   Can I get you anything . . .? Some tea?

Zoe   I'm okay, thanks . . . I already ate like a whole bag of cookies.

Kash   Oh . . . Look, this is gonna sound crazy, but I may have found a solution.

Zoe (*indifferent*)   Oh yeah? What's that?

Kash   Alright, so, I'm on my way back from the audition.

Zoe   Aw, shit, sorry. How'd it go?

Kash   It went.

Zoe   No fireworks?

Kash   It was a non-event. Director barely noticed I was in the room.

Zoe   Oh dear. I'm sorry, love –

Kash   Yeah, fuck it. Add another broken dream to the pile. Anyway, I'm walking to the tube, you know, wallowing in self-pity. I'm a terrible actor. I've chosen the wrong career. My life has no meaning, yadda yadda. But before I reach the station, I emerge momentarily from the fog of self-loathing, and it just so happens I'm standing outside a health-food shop. A massive fuck-off health-food superstore.

Zoe   Okay . . .?

Kash   So I figure: what the hell? I've got nowhere to be.
Nothing to do. Why don't I go inside, take a look for some
more supplements?

Zoe (*a disparaging sound*)   Pfff. You mean like the ones
you've been taking for months that make absolutely no
difference –

Kash (*ignoring her pessimism*)   I go into the shop, okay. Find
all the supplements and vitamins and shit. But I don't really
know what the hell I'm doing. What am I looking for?
Horny Goat Weed sounds like a good bet, but is it? Fuck
knows. I'm at a loss. And the shop assistant, he like clocks
me. Darts over with this dazzling smile. (*Shop assistant.*) 'Can
I help you, sir?' I'm thinking, fuck off, I'm not telling you
why I'm here. I've already been humiliated once today,
thank you very much, *but*, I dunno, somehow, we get talking.
We hit it off. Turns out *he*'s an actor too!

Zoe (*underwhelmed*)   Oh. Coincidence –

Kash   I know, right! What are the chances? Anyway, he
gives me his whole story. He's done loads of stuff. He's been
at the RSC. Has his own theatre company. He's a really nice
guy. Currently outta work. Been doing this shitty retail job
for a couple of months. Can't wait to get back onstage. I'm
like, I hear ya, brother. But while he's telling me all this,
already I'm thinking: something's going on here. Forces
beyond my mortal comprehension are at work. Destiny has
sent me a saviour!

Zoe (*sceptical*)   Right –

Kash   So now I figure: this dude's been honest with me.
He's told me *his* story. I might as well just open up. Explain
my situation to him.

Zoe   Uh, okay –?

Kash   So, that's what I do. I tell him: we've been trying for a baby. It's taking longer than we expected. Et cetera, et cetera –

Zoe   You told him that?

Kash   Not in a weird way. It was fine. We were totally on the same – (*Moving the story on quickly.*) Yeah, the point is: you'll never believe this. Guess how he responds. Guess what he tells me.

Zoe   What?

Kash   *He*'s been trying for a baby too!

Zoe (*still a little dubious*)   Really?

Kash   Yes! And not only that: it took him and his girlfriend like ten months of heartache and stress and fucking fertility plans and all the rest of it, BUT NOW SHE'S PREGNANT!

Zoe (*suddenly hopeful*)   Piss off!

Kash   I know! So, I'm like – Woah! My mind is blown here! This guy has been through exactly the same shit as us and he's come out the other side. He is now a fertility expert! He knows everything there is to know about these fucking supplements!

Zoe   Wow –

Kash   He talks me through all the options. I mean, pros, cons, side effects. Everything.

Zoe   Cool –

Kash   *But* – and this is where it really starts to get interesting . . .

Zoe   Go on . . .?

Kash   Trevor – that's his name – he kinda pulls me in close. Says, look, he's gonna level with me. All this shit, I keep taking it for long enough – eventually it might deliver. *It might.* But if we're serious, he says, if we really wanna conceive *now*, he's got a little something he can sell me under the counter at a very reasonable price. It will not fail –

Zoe (*her hope punctured again*)   Aw, fuck me. What have you bought?

Kash   No, no, listen, listen, Trevor and his wife, they used this – this miracle; within a few weeks, she's pregnant.

Zoe   What miracle? What have you done?

Kash *takes a small velvet pouch from his pocket and shows it to* **Zoe**.

Zoe   What the fuck is that? You bought some magic beans?

Kash (*opens the pouch*)   Take a look. See. Look inside.

Zoe   . . . What am I looking at? Can you just explain to me what the hell is going on?

Kash   Okay. Okay. Alright . . . How do I . . .? Okay! According to the Christian faith, what's the only part of Jesus Christ's body that did not ascend to heaven?

Zoe   . . . What are you talking about?

Kash   Just think about it. Please. Which part of Christ's earthly form did not go to heaven?

Zoe   I don't know . . .?

Kash   . . . His foreskin!

Zoe   . . .?

Kash   He was Jewish! He was circumcised! He left his foreskin behind!

Zoe   Why are you telling me this?!

Kash   Because. For centuries, Christ's foreskin has been a prized religious relic used to cure infertility.

Zoe   . . . I don't . . . I'm not . . . Are you saying you bought Jesus' foreskin?

Kash   Yes! No! Not all of it, obviously. Just a piece.

Zoe You bought a piece of Jesus Christ's foreskin from an unemployed actor in a fucking Holland & Barrett?!

Kash Yes! I mean, okay, it might not be the actual, historical foreskin –

Zoe How much?

Kash Huh?

Zoe How much did you pay for this – item?

Kash Not that much.

Zoe How much?

Kash It was a bargain.

Zoe How fucking much?

Kash . . . A hundred pounds.

Zoe A hundred pounds?! You gave away a hundred pounds –?

Kash Zoe, listen –

Zoe Show me the fucking – show it to me!

Kash Here. Look.

He shows **Zoe** *the 'foreskin'.*

Zoe That is not Jesus Christ's foreskin! That is a piece of leather!

Kash No, it's not –

Zoe You gave one hundred pounds to a strange man you only just met in return for a small piece of leather. What is the matter with you?

Kash Look, I understand your scepticism. I get it. I do. But please. You gotta give this a chance, Zo. Because it works, this thing. It really does. Trevor and his girlfriend –

Zoe   How? How does it work? What do you do? You put it under your pillow, do you? Before you have sex –

Kash   No, that's – that's not it –

Zoe   What then? What do you do?

Kash   . . . You eh – you chew it.

Zoe   I'm sorry?

Kash   You like – you chew the –

Zoe   You put it in your mouth?!

Kash   Yes.

Zoe   You want me to put a piece of circumcised foreskin that is apparently thousands of years old in my fucking mouth?

Kash   Well, not just you. Both of us. We gotta chew it to absorb its mystical properties.

Zoe   Oh my God! I can't – I can't even begin to – Are you fucking mental? Have you completely lost your shit? You're not even Christian –

Kash   I'm trying to help us, that's all! I thought you'd be pleased –

Zoe   Just shut the fuck up! Okay! Shut up! Seriously! Listen to me! Here's what's gonna happen: you're gonna go back to (*With disdain.*) Holland & Barrett. You're gonna return whatever the fuck that is, and you're gonna tell this Trevor – who is indeed, by the way, a fine actor – he's a fucking con artist – you're gonna demand a full refund from this crook and if he gives you any shit, you're gonna report him to the police. Do you understand? You need to go do that *now*, please. Fuck!

She exits –

Kash (*calls after her*)   Hold on, Zoe . . . Come back . . . Do you not think it's worth a try, at least . . .?

For a moment, **Kash** *is alone, deflated. But then* **Zoe** *returns.*

Zoe   Give it to me!

Kash   . . . What?

Zoe   Gimme the foreskin!

Kash   Why?

Zoe   Just give it to me!

Kash   What're you gonna do?

Zoe   I'm gonna chew it! Okay! You're right! It *is* worth a try!

Kash   Are you serious?

Zoe   Yes! I'm serious. Now gimme the fucking foreskin!

Kash   Here –

He hands the pouch to **Zoe***. She opens it and takes out the 'foreskin'.*

Kash   Are you sure about this?

Zoe *steels herself, closes her eyes and is about to put the 'foreskin' in her mouth when . . .*

There's a knock on the back door.

Kash   Oh my / God –

Zoe   Fuck! Seriously!

Kash   Are you expecting someone?

Zoe   No! Hang on.

She opens the door.

Naomi (*offstage, in the doorway*)   Hey.

Zoe   Oh. Hey.

Naomi (*offstage, in the doorway*)   Sorry. Is now a bad time?

Zoe   Eh, no –

Naomi (*offstage, in the doorway*)   You mind if I come in a minute?

Zoe   . . . Sure, yeah. Come on in –

Naomi *enters.*

Kash   Hey, Naomi.

Naomi   Hey, love. Sorry to –

Kash   No –

Naomi   I need to ask a favour.

Zoe   Of course . . . What's up?

Naomi   . . .

Kash   Eh, I should prob'ly –

Naomi   Oh – Is that –?

Kash   No, that's – yeah. I'll – No problem. I might head out actually. (*To* **Zoe**, *re the 'foreskin'.*) Eh, should I take the –?

Zoe   No, leave it with me.

Kash   Okay, eh . . . so I'm not bringing it back to / the –?

Zoe   Just, go on, would you? / We'll talk later –

Kash   No. Fine. Fine. Let's – yeah.

He exits.

Naomi (*re the 'foreskin'*)   What is that?

Zoe   I couldn't begin to tell you.

Naomi   Oh –

Zoe (*puts the 'foreskin' in her pocket*)   Anyway, what's going on?

Naomi   Eh, okay, so . . . I've done it. I've left him.

Zoe   . . . As in . . .?

Naomi   I've left Charlie. I stayed at a B&B last night.

Zoe   No?

Naomi   I'm serious.

Zoe   Jesus. Eh. What happened?

Naomi   Ah, nothing dramatic. I've just had enough, you know. I'm done. I can't be around him anymore.

Zoe   Wow. Okay.

Naomi   Also I shagged someone else.

Zoe   What?!

Naomi   I – Yeah.

Zoe   Woah. Fuck. That's . . .

Naomi   Bad. I know –

Zoe   Who? Not someone from school?

Naomi   No! God. No. Give me some credit.

Zoe   Well, who then? Do I know him?

Naomi (*shakes her head*)   . . . You won't believe me if I tell you.

Zoe   You have to tell me.

Naomi   . . .

Zoe   Gimme a name at least.

Naomi   You'll laugh.

Zoe   I'm not gonna laugh at his name –

Naomi   Rocco. His name is Rocco.

Zoe   . . . Rocco?

Naomi *nods*.

Zoe (*suppressing a laugh*)   You had sex with a man called Rocco?

Naomi   Yes.

Zoe   What is he like a porn star?

Naomi   No. Shut up. He's not a porn star. He's a personal trainer.

Zoe   . . . How did you meet a personal trainer?

Naomi   At the gym.

Zoe   You hate the gym.

Naomi   I know! I go one time. I end up shagging a fucking personal trainer.

Zoe   Are you messing with me? Is this like –?

Naomi   No! Okay, look, I'll just – I'll lay it out, alright. Tuesday evening, I go to the gym. For the first time in my life. I walk in. I don't know what to expect. Turns out it's like a weird sex dungeon. Honestly. All these machines. Floor-to-ceiling mirrors. Men lifting things. I'm like what the fuck? I haven't had sex in over a year. This is not where I need to be. But okay. I hop on the cross-trainer. And I try to like 'work on my cardio'. But it's fucking impossible to concentrate. There are semi-naked hunks everywhere. *Working out*. All sweaty and panting. And there's this one . . . man. This one *highly attractive* man . . .

Zoe   How highly attractive?

Naomi   Fucking gorgeous. Looks like an actor or something. Not like Kash. A real actor. A movie star! Only: shorts. Vest. Muscles –

Zoe   Fuck –

Naomi   I can't keep my eyes off him –

Zoe (*agreement*)   No –

Naomi   And, by some miraculous turn, when he sees me looking at him, *he starts looking back at me* –

Zoe   Holy shit –

Naomi   Giving me the, you know: 'I want you' –

Zoe   No –?

Naomi   Which, I'm literally trying not to orgasm on the spot –

Zoe   Jesus –

Naomi   So I get off the machine. We get talking. Before I know it . . . In the back of my car, in the Sainsbury's car park.

Zoe   . . . What?!

Naomi   Yep –

Zoe   You had sex in the back of your car –?

Naomi   Uh-huh –

Zoe   In the Sainsbury's car park?

Naomi   That is correct.

Zoe   No, you didn't!

Naomi   I did! I really did!

Zoe   That is insane!

Naomi   Yeah, but you should see this man. He's like twenty years younger than me and he is an immortal sex god!

Zoe   Woah. This is . . .

She gestures and makes the sound of her head exploding –

Naomi   I know. It's so wrong. So wrong. Charlie would like . . .

Zoe   Hang on. Does Charlie know?

Naomi   No. Are you mad? No. (*Beat.*) I need a place to stay, Zo.

Zoe   . . . You can stay here.

Naomi   Really?

Zoe   We got a spare room.

Naomi   Oh my God –

Zoe   It's yours for as long as you need it –

Naomi   Woman, you are the best.

Zoe   It's no big deal.

Naomi   I know you got your own shit to deal with –

Zoe   It's fine.

Naomi   Kash won't mind?

Zoe   Kash'll be fine. Honestly. It's not a problem.

Naomi   Thank you.

Zoe   Where's your stuff?

Naomi   Outside. In the car.

Zoe   Oh. Okay –

Naomi   Sorry –

Zoe   No. Go grab what you need. Come back. We'll talk some more.

Naomi   You're sure it's okay?

Zoe   Positive.

Naomi   Thanks, love. Thank you . . . I'll be back in a few minutes.

Zoe   Alright.

Naomi *exits.* **Zoe** *exhales. Beat. She takes the 'foreskin' from her pocket. She looks at it. She puts it in her mouth and starts to chew cautiously, exploratively, as if waiting for some magic to happen, when –*

Blackout.

Scene Four

The next morning.

Sex noises. **Zoe** *and* **Kash** *are mid-argument.*

Kash   I just think you could've spoken to me first.

Zoe   She's my friend. She's upset. What do you expect me
to do –?

Naomi (*offstage*)   Oh God, that feels so good.

Kash   Yeah, she sounds upset. She sounds devastated. Shall
I go offer her some comfort?

Zoe   Are you sure that's not the neighbours?

Kash   It's not the neighbours. Are you crazy? It's her.

Zoe   Well, whatever. She needs a place to stay. You'll just
have to get over it.

Kash   What about our . . .?

Zoe   Our what?

Kash   You know . . . our efforts to conceive? The fertility
plan?

Zoe   What about it?

Kash   We'll have to take a break.

Zoe   Why?

Naomi (*offstage*)   Don't stop. Oh don't stop –

Kash   Because. She'll hear us.

Zoe   We'll do it while she's out.

Kash   That hardly seems fair. It's our flat.

Zoe   We're not taking a break.

Kash   Well, I'm not having sex while she's in the house.

Zoe   Like I said: we'll do it while she's out.

Kash   It's ridiculous . . . You need to speak to her.

Naomi (*offstage*)   Talk to me. Talk dirty to me –

Zoe   About what?

Kash   The noises.

Zoe   I'm not gonna do that.

Kash   Why not?

Zoe   It'd be . . . awkward.

Kash   Well, I don't wanna listen to it.

Naomi (*offstage*)   Yes, just like that! Just like that –

Zoe   That definitely sounds like the neighbours to me.

Kash   It's not the fucking neighbours, Zoe. Would you get real?

Zoe (*'don't be so pissy'*)   Okay. Alright.

Kash   . . . Have you met this Rocco, by the way?

Zoe   Yes. Have you?

Kash   Hmm, let me think. I've seen him at the gym a couple of times. But this morning, out of nowhere, he walks in on me in the bathroom!

Zoe   Oh –

Kash   Imagine my fucking surprise!

Zoe   Did you get a fright?

Kash   Yes! I did!

Zoe   I'm sorry.

Naomi (*offstage*)   Harder! Harder –

Kash   To add to the fucking mortification of it: when he walked in, I was doing a sit-down wee-wee!

Zoe *struggles to contain her laughter.*

Kash   Why are you laughing?

Zoe   I'm not. Sorry. I'm not. Why were you doing a sit-down wee-wee?

Naomi (*offstage*)   Faster! Faster –

Kash   So as not to get any splashes on the toilet seat.

Zoe   Aw, that is so thoughtful.

Kash   Yeah, well, now he thinks I'm some sort of effeminate woman pisser.

Zoe   He prob'ly thinks you were doing a poo.

Kash   Oh even better –

Naomi (*offstage*)   / Don't stop –

Zoe   You're allowed to take a poo in your own house.

Kash   Apparently, I'm not. Not without a visitor from the gym popping in for a quick inspection.

Zoe   You're being silly now.

Kash   Just talk to her, please.

Zoe   No. You'll just have to block it out –

Naomi (*offstage, climaxing*)   Oh God! Oh God! OHHHHHH GOD YES!

Kash   How am I supposed to block that out?

Zoe   Don't listen to it.

Kash   Gosh, what a helpful suggestion! Thank you. (*Sincere.*) Maybe I'll speak to her myself.

Zoe   You will not!

Kash   Well, if you're not gonna do it . . .

Zoe   You're not speaking to her. No way. She's my friend. She's welcome here.

Kash   She's welcome to have loud Olympic sex marathons, is she . . .? (*Off her look.*) Yes, she is! Fine. I won't speak to her. In fact, maybe I'll invite some other random strangers round to our flat for a gang-bang!

Zoe   Why are you being like this?

Kash   I'm not being like anything. I just don't wanna listen to other people having sex . . . What if she's at home during the window?

Zoe   You're overthinking this, Kash. Seriously.

Kash   . . . I just wish you'd spoken to me first.

Zoe   I'm sorry. Okay. Genuinely. I am.

Kash   . . . Apology accepted. Reluctantly.

Zoe   Thank you.

Kash   How long is she likely to stay anyway?

Zoe   We haven't discussed that yet.

Rocco *enters, wearing only a pair of boxer shorts, sweat glistening on his naked torso.*

Rocco   Hey, guys.

Zoe   Morning, Rocco.

Rocco   Mind if I grab a glass of water?

Zoe   No. Not at all.

Kash (*bitter*)   Make yourself at home.

Rocco   Thank you. Bare thirsty.

He gets a glass of water. **Zoe** *and* **Kash** *watch as* **Rocco** *guzzles the water down in one before putting the glass in the sink.*

Rocco   Well, better get back.

Zoe   Of course.

Rocco   I really appreciate your hospitality, guys.

Zoe   You're very welcome.

Rocco   Safe. Chat soon.

He exits.

Zoe   See. He's perfectly pleasant.

Kash   Those were my boxers!

Zoe   What?

Kash   He was wearing my boxer shorts!

Zoe   Don't be ridiculous.

Kash   He was!

Zoe   They weren't your boxers.

Kash   That is fucking outrageous. What kind of lowlife steals another man's boxer shorts?

Zoe   He didn't steal anything –

Kash   I'll have to speak to him. In fact, yeah, I'm gonna speak to him right now. Man to man. Get a few things straight –

Zoe   You're not going to speak him.

Kash   Yes, I am.

Zoe   Would you just fucking stop?! Please!

Kash   . . . Alright. You don't need to raise your voice.

Zoe   Apparently, I do!

Kash   . . . I'll speak to him later.

Zoe   You won't speak to him at all!

Kash   Fine.

Beat. The sex noises resume – but this time from the upstairs flat. **Zoe** *and* **Kash** *look up at the ceiling – then at each other –*

Kash   *That* is the neighbours.

Blackout.

Scene Five

A few weeks later.

Kash *enters purposefully. He searches for something. After a moment –*

Kash (*calls out*)   Zo . . .? Zoe . . .?

Zoe (*offstage*)   . . . What?

Kash (*calls out*)   . . . Where are you?

Zoe (*offstage*)   I'm on the fucking toilet!

Kash   Oh. Right. (*Calls out.*) Sorry.

Zoe (*offstage*)   What's wrong?

Kash (*calls out*)   Nothing. Just. Can't find my phone.

Zoe (*offstage*)   . . . You want me to call it?

Kash (*calls out*)   Eh, yeah, would you?

Zoe (*offstage*)   Gimme a second.

He waits. Nothing happens.

Zoe (*offstage*)   Are we alone?

Kash (*calls out*)   Huh?

Zoe (*offstage*)   Is Naomi home?

Kash (*calls out*)   No. It's just us. I'm not having sex though. My penis is destroyed.

He waits again. Still nothing.

Kash (*calls out*)   Is it ringing?

Zoe (*offstage*)   I haven't called it yet.

Kash   Oh . . .

He waits some more.

(*Calls out.*) Have you called it now –?

Zoe (*offstage*)   I don't actually know where *my* phone is either.

Kash   For fuck's sake. (*Calls out.*) Fine. Don't worry about it.

He resumes his search.

Zoe (*offstage*)   Hey, can I tell you something?

Kash (*calls out*)   Yes.

Zoe (*offstage*)   I knew all along I hadn't got my phone.

Kash (*calls out*)   . . . What?

Zoe (*offstage*)   I was fucking with you! Hope you find it though. (*Mock sweetness and light.*) Love you.

Kash (*calls out*)   Love you.

He continues to look for his phone. After a moment, somewhere in the room, the phone buzzes. He stops. Beat.

Kash (*calls out*)   Did you just message me?

Zoe (*offstage*)   . . . No.

He still can't find the phone.

Kash (*calls out*)   You did!

Zoe (*offstage, mischievous*)   Did I?

Kash (*calls out*)   Can you just call my phone please?

Zoe (*offstage*)   I told you: I don't know where *my* phone is.

His phone buzzes again.

Kash (*calls out, semi-amused*)   You're an asshole, do you know that? (*Finds the phone, calls out.*) Ah! Hah! Fuck you! Found it!

He picks up the phone. He checks an email.

Kash (*calls out*)   Twelve o'clock.

Zoe (*offstage*)   . . . What's that?

Kash (*calls out*)   My meeting. It's at twelve.

No response.

Kash (*calls out*)   You asked me to tell you . . .

No response. Beat. He opens the messages she has just sent him.

Kash (*calls out*)   Hey, why you sending me pictures of a –

Zoe *enters, barefoot, in pyjamas or a dressing gown, a pregnancy test in her hand, a massive smile on her face.*

Kash   – pregnancy test?

Zoe (*self-service checkout voice*)   'Unexpected item in the bagging area.'

Beat.

Kash   No?

Zoe   Yes!

Kash   No?

Zoe   Yes!

Kash   You're shitting me?!

Zoe   I've never been more serious about anything in my whole life!

Kash   But, like –

Zoe   I know –

Kash   Like –

Zoe   I know!

Kash   . . . I can't – I don't – Are you sure?

Zoe   I've done four of these bad boys!

Kash   What?!

Zoe (*waves the pregnancy test at him*)   Uno. (*Removes another pregnancy test from her dressing gown.*) Dos. (*And another.*) Tres. (*And another.*) Cuatro –

Kash   Holy fuck –

Zoe   All said the same beautiful thing! Look! Two lines . . .

Kash   Oh my God! Oh my God! This is – How?! How did this happen?

Zoe   Well, I think *someone* owes Trevor an apology.

Kash   The holy foreskin!

Zoe   I'm kidding! I'm kidding! It's nothing to do with the foreskin. This is all us.

Kash   We're having a baby?

Zoe   We're having a baby, motherfucker!

Kash   Fuck yeah!

Zoe   Come here.

They hug.

Zoe   Are you okay?

Kash   I'm . . . yeah. Are *you* okay? That's the –

Zoe   I'm fine. I'm good.

Kash   How do you feel? Do you feel different?

Zoe   I just feel . . . happy.

Kash   How are your breasts?

Zoe   What?

Kash   Are your nipples sore?

Zoe   Why would my nipples be sore?

Kash   I dunno. I think that's what happens. Look, we need to get you some folic acid. And like a manicure. And a pedicure. / And –

Zoe (*moves away*)   Would you fuck off? Don't start fussing.

Kash   What you doing?

Zoe   You'll see.

She grabs his phone.

Kash   What?

Zoe   Celebrating.

Kash   Oh no –

Zoe   I think you know what's happening here.

Kash   I think I do.

Zoe *presses 'Play' on the phone and the opening of 'I Really Like You' by Carly Rae Jepson leaps from the wifi speaker, filling the room.* **Zoe** *starts to sing and dance, beckoning* **Kash** *to join her. He soon does. They move together, joyfully, unselfconsciously, sharing a moment of pure giddy elation and excitement. They know all the words of the song. They've sung it together before – but never quite like this. We get at least the first chorus before –*

Blackout.

Scene Six

Later the same day.

Naomi *and* **Charlie** *are at the kitchen table.*

Naomi   How are you?

Charlie   Fine . . . How are you?

Naomi   Fine.

Short pause.

Naomi   How's the (*pointed*) tea room?

Charlie   Good. Thank you.

Naomi   . . . Business is . . .?

Charlie   Business is good, yeah.

Naomi   Good . . . Good . . .

Beat.

Naomi   I've been stealing cakes.

Charlie   . . . What?

Naomi   I have a key. I let myself in. Late at night. When you're not there. I steal cakes.

Charlie   . . . Oh.

Naomi   Sorry.

Charlie   . . . It's okay.

Naomi   It's not really.

Charlie   . . . I did wonder actually. Thought I might be going mad.

Naomi   No. Just me. Cake thief.

Charlie   Right.

Naomi   . . . You want the key back . . .?

Charlie   Keep it. (*Off her look.*) In case I lose mine, or . . .

Naomi   Sure.

Beat.

Charlie   I don't really understand what's happening here.

Naomi   What do you mean?

Charlie   Us. I don't understand what's happening – to us.

Naomi   . . . Our marriage is ending.

Charlie   Why?

Naomi   Seriously . . .? You want me to explain why?

Charlie   Yes. I do.

Naomi   I don't like the sound you make when you breathe.

Charlie   . . . Sorry?

Naomi   When you breathe – you make this – sound. This annoying sound. Pisses me right off.

Charlie   . . . What sound?

Naomi   Just – a sound. A breathing sound. It's fucking irritating.

Charlie   . . . And that's the reason our marriage is ending –?

Naomi   Yes.

Charlie   That's the decisive / factor –

Naomi   That's the only reason.

Charlie   Okay –

Naomi   It's nothing to do with the fact that you have paid me no attention for as long as I can remember. You have no interest in me. We have no common interests. We never do anything together. We *never* have sex. *Ever.* None of those things are important. It's all about the fucking infuriating breathing sound.

Charlie *shakes his head, struggling for a moment to articulate something massive, but in the end all he comes up with is –*

Charlie   Fine.

Beat.

Have you spoken to Jada?

Naomi   Yes.

Charlie   Have you told her?

Naomi   No.

Charlie   You said you were gonna tell her.

Naomi   I know I did. I will.

Charlie   When?

Naomi   Soon.

Beat.

Charlie   She's coming home at the weekend.

Naomi   She said.

Charlie   I think you should be there.

Naomi   Where?

Charlie   At the house.

Naomi   Why?

Charlie   Because. If she comes home and you're not there, you're just gone, don't you think that'd be a little – messed up?

Naomi   . . . I'll be there.

Charlie   Good. You can talk to her then. We can both talk to her. Together.

Naomi   Sure.

Charlie   Okay.

Beat.

Naomi   That it?

Charlie   Guess so.

Naomi   Right. I'll see you Friday evening then. I'll be there on Friday evening.

Charlie   Friday evening.

He goes to leave – but stops. Beat.

You could stay . . .

Naomi   . . . What?

Charlie   You could stay home. Not come back / here –

Naomi   Charlie, please –

Charlie   You wouldn't have to talk to her at all then. You wouldn't have to tell her. You could just come home. Everything could go back to normal –

Naomi   That can't happen –

Charlie   We could see a counsellor.

Naomi   I don't wanna see a counsellor.

Charlie   We could get a dog.

Naomi   Charlie –

Charlie   I'm not allergic. Not really. That was – I wasn't serious –

Naomi   I'm not coming back, Charlie! Alright! I'm not coming back!

Charlie   Why not?

Naomi   I told you why.

Charlie   Have you met someone?

Naomi   . . .

Charlie   Have you?

Naomi   No.

Charlie   You have.

Naomi   I haven't met anyone –

Charlie   You're lying.

Naomi   I'm not lying –

Charlie   You *are*. I can tell –

Naomi   I don't love you! Okay! That's why I can't come back! I don't love you! I don't remember ever loving you! I certainly don't love you now!

Beat.

Charlie   Gimme the key.

Naomi   What?

Charlie   The key to the tea room – I want it back.

Naomi (*gives him back the key*)   Here. All yours.

Charlie   You're gonna break Jada's heart, you know that?

Naomi   . . .

Charlie   You don't care.

Naomi   Fuck you –

Charlie   You don't give a toss about anyone but yourself . . .

He glowers at her. She refuses to meet his gaze.

He exits via the back door. She's alone, rattled.

Blackout.

Scene Seven

A few weeks later.

The kitchen is empty. **Zoe** *rushes in and vomits into the sink.*

Zoe (*groans*)   Ughhh Jesus . . .

For a moment, she remains hunched over the basin. Then she heaves her head up. She runs the tap to clean the mess. Eventually, she sits down at the kitchen table, miserable.

Offstage, the main door of the flat opens and shuts. We hear someone whistling cheerfully. Soon after, the whistler enters: it's **Kash**, *carrying a shopping bag.*

Kash (*ebullient*)   Good morning, wifey!

Zoe (*grunts*)   Unhh.

Kash *puts the shopping down.*

Kash (*addresses* **Zoe**'s *stomach*)   And good morning to you, my son and heir! How are you today? (*Cupping his ear to* **Zoe**'s *stomach, then telling her 'what the fetus has said'.*) . . . He says he's very well because he has the best mummy in the whole wide world.

Zoe (*another grunt*)   / Guhhh –

Kash (*addresses* **Zoe**'s *stomach*)   I thoroughly agree. (*Cupping his ear to her stomach again.*) What . . .? What's that you say . . .? You want me to recite Shakespeare to you?!

Zoe (*limp protest*)   / Kash –

Kash (*to* **Zoe**'s *stomach, mock reluctance*)   Not again! (*To* **Zoe**.) This child is a genius.

Zoe   Please –

Kash (*with gusto*)   'Once more unto the breach, dear friends, once more; or close the wall up with our English dead.'

Zoe   Stop.

Kash   Oh come on, my love! It's a beautiful day! What're your plans?!

Zoe   Sleep.

Kash (*silly voice*)   Sleep, motherfucker! (*Normal voice.*) You don't wanna go out somewhere together?

Zoe   No.

Kash   No. Okay. Sleep it is, then. Of course, if you like, I could join you in the bedroom. We could have a little *sexy time*.

Zoe   . . . I'm not having sex with you.

Kash   No? May I enquire why?

Zoe   I have neither the energy nor the desire. I just vomited in the sink –

Kash   Oh. Shit –

Zoe   I never want to have sex again.

Kash   Did you know many women, in fact, have an increased sex drive during the first trimester . . .? But not you. Which is fine.

Zoe   . . . Have you been to the shops?

Kash   I have.

Zoe   You didn't get any paracetamol, did you?

Kash   No. I'll go back and get some.

Zoe   Thank you. I need some other stuff as well.

Kash   Hold on. Lemme make a list.

He finds a pen and picks up **Zoe**'s *notebook.*

Kash   You mind if I tear a page out of your notebook?

Zoe   Go ahead.

Beat. Something written in the notebook has caught **Kash**'s *attention.*

Kash   What's this?

Zoe   What's what?

Kash   It's like a list of baby stuff. With like prices and shit.

Zoe   Oh. Yeah. We need to buy some things. We'll talk about it later –

Kash (*a sudden outburst of incredulity/despair*)   A grand and a half for a pushchair!

Zoe   Unless you wanna talk about it now?

Kash   I think we should. Yes.

Zoe   Okay. Show me the . . .

He shows her the notebook.

Zoe   Right. First off. It's not a just pushchair. It's a travel system. Pushchair. Carry cot. Car seat and base.

Kash   We don't have a car, Zoe.

Zoe   Yeah, we're gonna have to get one.

Kash   Fuck! Look at all this shit. Baby monitor. Baby carrier. Baby bath. Changing mat. Changing table. Cot. Moses basket. Breast pump. Breast pads –

Zoe   We need everything on this list, love. Sorry. We do.

Kash   How we gonna pay for it?

Zoe   . . . I didn't wanna spring it on you like this.

Kash   Spring what on me like what?

Zoe   . . . You're gonna have to get a job.

Kash   . . . I have a job.

Zoe   I mean a real job.

Kash   Acting is a real job.

Zoe   A real job with a regular, reliable salary.

Kash   Ah, Zoe, come on, if I'd known that . . .

Zoe   What?

Kash   . . . Nothing. Aw, this is terrible. There must be some other way?

Zoe   I dunno what to tell you. We need money coming in every month from both of us . . . I'll be on leave as well, remember. Maternity pay – it's fuck-all.

Kash   Oh my God.

Zoe   Sorry. (*Beat.*) You gonna go to the shop for me then or what?

Kash   We can't afford it.

Zoe   Don't be silly. Go on.

Kash . . . You know what, just text me the list.

Zoe Eh, okay . . . Hey . . . I'm not saying you need to give up acting completely . . . We'll figure it out. I promise.

Kash *smiles weakly then exits.*

Zoe (*hit by a sudden wave of nausea*) Oh no –

She rushes to the sink again.

Blackout.

Scene Eight

A few weeks later.

Naomi *bursts into the kitchen in underwear and kimono. She opens drawers and cupboards, hastily searching for something. After a short time,* **Rocco** *enters in his boxer shorts.*

Rocco Any luck?

Naomi No. You?

Rocco No.

Naomi Fuck.

Rocco Is there like a drawer of random shit?

Naomi (*opens drawer*) Yeah. Here. Look. I can't see any in there. People don't keep condoms in the kitchen, do they?

Rocco No –

Naomi If they're anywhere, they'll be in the bedroom.

Rocco Are you suggesting what I think you're suggesting?

Naomi What do you think I'm suggesting?

Rocco We perform a cheeky little condom raid.

Naomi Zoe and Kash are in the bedroom.

Rocco So . . .?

Naomi   We can't go in there.

Rocco   I'm light on my feet, fam. Like a ninja. They'll never notice.

Naomi   Just go to the shops and buy a pack.

Rocco   You want me to go *all the way* to the shops and *all the way* back again?

Naomi   Yes.

Rocco   Can you really wait that long?

Naomi   I'm not sure I can.

They kiss.

Naomi (*pulls away*)   Oh God. Go. Hurry.

Rocco   I'll get my clothes.

Naomi *opens another drawer.*

Naomi (*slams the drawer shut*)   Oh fuck.

Beat.

Rocco   What?

Naomi *opens the drawer and quickly slams it shut again.*

Naomi   Shit!

Rocco   What is it?!

Naomi   I just saw something I don't think I'm supposed to see.

Rocco   What?!

Naomi   I prob'ly shouldn't say.

Rocco   Is it naked photos?

Naomi   No!

Rocco   What then?

Naomi   Oh Jesus –

Naomi *opens the drawer again. She takes out a pregnancy scan and shows it to* **Rocco**.

Rocco (*'shit, this is big'*)   . . . Ohhhhhh . . . Zoe . . .?

Naomi *nods.*

Rocco   Shiiiiiitttt!

Naomi   What do I do?

Rocco   Wait so, this was –?

Naomi   It was just lying there – on top of the –

Rocco   But she hasn't told you –?

Naomi   No. I'm obviously not supposed to know. What do I do?

Rocco   Put it back. Pretend you never saw it.

Naomi   Really?

Rocco   One hundred per cent. If she ain't ready to tell you yet, you gotta respect that, innit.

Naomi   Okay. Yes. You're right. God. You really like make me a better person.

Rocco   And you me.

They kiss, with **Naomi** *still holding the pregnancy scan. The kiss grows more passionate, until* **Zoe** *enters (her bump starting to show for the first time).*

Zoe   Hey, guys –

The kiss ends abruptly –

Naomi (*jumps*)   Yow! What the fuck!

She reels away, hiding the scan behind her back.

Zoe (*freezes*)   . . . Eh, hello . . . Is everything okay?

Naomi   Yes. Sorry. Yes. Everything is okay. Indeed. Absolutely. Completely. Total okay-ness.

Zoe   . . . I was just gonna make some tea.

Naomi   Okay. Sure. Tea. Yes. Good choice.

Beat.

Zoe   What's going on?

Naomi   Nothing.

Zoe   Were you two having sex in here?

Naomi   Eh –

Rocco   / Yes!

Naomi   No!

Zoe   Wait, you were?!

Naomi   / Yes –

Rocco   No –

Zoe   Naomi, be honest with me: were you or were you not having sex in my kitchen?

Naomi   Were we having sex in her kitchen?

Rocco   . . . Just tell her the truth.

Naomi   But you said not to tell her the truth –

Zoe   What truth?

Rocco   It's too late. Just tell her.

Naomi   Alright. Fuck it. Look . . .

She shows the pregnancy scan to **Zoe** –

Naomi   We found this.

Zoe   . . . Oh . . . You –?

Naomi   It was in the drawer.

Rocco   We were looking for condoms.

Naomi   She doesn't need to know that, honey –

Rocco   No, of course –

Naomi   I'm so sorry –

Zoe   It's okay –

Naomi   I found it. I panicked. I didn't know what to do –

Zoe   It's fine . . . Actually, I've wanted to tell you for weeks.

Naomi   Oh my God! You're pregnant!

Zoe   I know!

Naomi   Come here!

Zoe *and* **Naomi** *hug one another.*

Naomi   I am so pleased for you –

Rocco   Congratulations –

Zoe   Thank you. Thank you.

Naomi   What are you – twelve weeks?

Zoe   Thirteen weeks and two days.

Naomi   Wow.

Rocco   How are you feeling?

Zoe   I'm alright –

Kash (*offstage*)   Zoe –

Zoe   I've had some bad nausea.

Naomi   Oh no –

Zoe   But I think it's starting to ease off now. At least, I hope it is –

Rocco   It usually does after the first trimester.

Zoe   . . . Do you have much pregnancy experience, Rocco?

Rocco   My sisters all got kids, innit –

Kash *enters, wearing a barista uniform.*

Kash (*as he enters*)   You haven't seen my little badge, have you? (*Sees* **Naomi** *and* **Rocco**.) Oh, hi, everyone.

Naomi *starts to sing 'Big Spender' which continues throughout the following:*

Zoe   What badge?

Kash   My name badge.

Zoe   No, sorry.

Rocco   What's with the costume, mate? You in a play?

Kash (*irritated*)   No –

Zoe   It's not a costume. It's the uniform for his new job.

Rocco   Oh –

Rocco   I'm confused. Have you given up the acting then?

Kash   No, I haven't given up *the acting* –

Zoe   We just need a little extra cash –

Kash   Why is she singing –?

Zoe   She, eh – she knows –

Kash   She knows what –?

Zoe   She *knows* –

Naomi   I *know*, Kashif. Or should I call you – *Daddy*?

Kash *looks at* **Zoe**, *horrified.*

Kash   She knows?

Zoe   She found the scan.

Naomi (*holding the scan*)   Exhibit A!

Kash   Oh –

Rocco   We were looking for condoms, bruv. Sorry. Total accident.

Naomi   Gimme a cuddle!

She hugs **Kash**.

Naomi   Well played, my friend. Well played.

Kash   Thank you.

Naomi   How you feeling?

Kash   I'm fine –

Naomi *starts to sing 'A Whole New World'.*

Kash   Is she gonna do this all day?

Naomi   I'm excited for you! That's all! Hey, why don't I make us all a meal tonight? The four of us. In honour of the new arrival.

Zoe   That'd be lovely.

Naomi   Just tell me one thing, both of you. Boy or girl . . .? Which would you prefer?

Zoe   . . . Either –

Kash   I'm easy.

Naomi   Oh come on –

Zoe   He wants a boy.

Kash   I never said that.

Zoe   Yes, you did.

Kash   When?

Zoe   He's desperate for a boy.

Kash   I am not desperate for a boy –

Rocco   Show me the thing. I'll tell you now.

They all look at **Rocco**.

Rocco   . . . Show me the scan. I'll tell you right now whether the baby is a boy or a girl.

Still they look at **Rocco**, *incredulous.*

Rocco   . . . All my sisters got kids . . .

Kash   And . . .?

Rocco   If you wanna know, I can tell you.

Naomi   May I . . .?

Zoe's *phone rings.*

Zoe   Sure.

Kash (*dismissive*)   Whatever.

Zoe (*re the phone*)   Sorry. I gotta take this.

She exits, while **Naomi** *gives* **Rocco** *the pregnancy scan.*

Kash   You can't tell the sex from that image.

Rocco (*studies the scan*)   *I* can.

Kash   It's impossible. The sex organs are not visible.

Rocco   Not to the untrained eye.

Kash   Oh, and you have a trained eye, do you?

Rocco   Yes, I do.

Kash   What, you're a qualified midwife? You're a sonographer?

Rocco   Let's just say I spend a lot of time at the maternity unit with my contraception-averse sisters.

Kash   You're full of shit –

Rocco   That – if I am not mistaken, and I rarely am – that, ladies and gentlemen, is a boy.

Kash (*suddenly excited*)   No way!

Rocco   Look. (*Shows the scan to* **Kash**.) Arms. Legs. Stomach. Penis.

Kash   . . . Oh my God, he's right!

Naomi   Really?!

Kash (*calls out*)   Zoe, we're having a boy –

Naomi   Show me. I wanna see –

Rocco (*shows* **Naomi** *the scan*)   Right there. See. That's a penis.

Naomi   That's not a penis!

Rocco   Yes, it is!

Kash   That's a penis!

Naomi   No, it's not.

Rocco   What is it if it's not a penis?

Naomi   It's a shadow.

Rocco   It's not a shadow!

Kash   It's a penis! It's a definite penis! I knew it! I told her! I knew it was gonna be a boy!

Naomi   I don't think you can say that –

Rocco   Trust me, you can –

Kash (*grandly*)   Kashif and son!

Naomi   Okay, a minute ago you were Mr Cautious –

Kash (*exaggerated Cockney accent*)   I'm going down the pub with my son.

Naomi   Now you're taking your infant son to the pub –

Kash (*same*)   'Me and my son, yeah, we come to the Arsenal *every* Saturday.'

Rocco   Wait, are you a Gooner –?

Kash   Yes!

Naomi   Oh Christ, / they're gonna start talking about football –

Rocco   Oh my days, man!

Kash   You an' all?

Rocco   Yes, bruv! Long-suffering!

Kash   No way –

Naomi   Rocco, you were gonna go to the shops, weren't you?

Rocco   Yeah, I'm just chatting with my boy here!

Zoe *returns, stunned.*

Kash   Zoe, hey, look, check it out! It's a boy! Our baby is a boy! Rocco, mate, show her the scan –

Naomi   What's wrong?

Beat.

Zoe   There's a problem.

Naomi   What?

Kash   What problem?

Zoe   I need you to come with me to the hospital.

Kash   What're you talking about? What's the matter?

Zoe   There's a problem with the baby.

Naomi   Oh / fuck –

Kash   What sorta problem? I don't understand.

Zoe   I don't understand either. I don't know what she said to me.

Kash   Who? Who did you talk to –?

Zoe   The midwife.

Kash   Okay, so lemme call her back. I'll talk to her. I'll sort it out.

Zoe   You're not hearing me. We need to go to the hospital now.

Kash   But – but that's – Everything is – I'm supposed to be at work in an hour.

Zoe   Fine. I'll go on my own then.

Kash   What? No –

Zoe *exits.*

Kash   Hold on. Zoe. (*Turns to* **Naomi** *and* **Rocco**.) What the fuck?

Naomi   Go after her, for God's sake.

Kash   Shit! (*Calls out.*) Zoe . . .

He rushes out. **Naomi** *and* **Rocco** *look at one another.*

Blackout.

Act Two

Scene One

Later the same day.

Charlie *has recently arrived in the kitchen. He hands* **Naomi** *a bag.*

Charlie   I, eh – I brought some of your stuff.

Naomi   What stuff?

Charlie   From the house. Woman's stuff. Lotions and creams and whatnot. Thought it might come in handy.

Naomi   You didn't need to do that.

Charlie   Well, you know me. Generous to a fault.

Naomi (*cold*)   Mmm. Thanks.

She puts the bag on the table.

Charlie   No problem. Any time . . . I was thinking, you see. Must be hard for you here. You know, roughing it.

Naomi (*sharp*)   I'm fine.

Charlie   Zoe looking after you?

Naomi   I'm looking after myself.

Charlie   Good. Good . . . You're keeping well then?

Naomi   Yes.

He looks at her expectantly.

Charlie   This is the part where you ask how I'm doing.

Naomi (*ostentatiously bored*)   How are you doing –?

Charlie   Not too great actually. As it happens. No.

Naomi (*same*)   Why's that?

Charlie Just struggling on all fronts really. Since you left. Can't eat. Can't sleep. Can't concentrate. And there's been a lot of bad shit going down at the house. Multiple domestic emergencies.

Naomi Like what?

Charlie Well, the washing machine's busted.

Naomi That constitutes an emergency, does it?

Charlie I got no clean clothes.

Naomi So, go to the laundrette.

Charlie I might have to, yeah.

Naomi Is the machine actually busted, or do you just not know how to use it?

Charlie (*gentle protest*)   Hey now.

Naomi (*sighs, shakes her head*)   . . . What else?

Charlie Huh?

Naomi You said multiple emergencies . . .?

Charlie (*thinks*)   . . . That's all I can remember.

Naomi Jesus wept. Call a plumber.

Charlie I have.

Naomi Okay. Great. Anything else I can help you with? Cos I got shit to do / here –

Charlie Open the bag.

Naomi What?

Charlie The bag. Open it. Look inside.

Naomi *is reluctant.*

Charlie Open the bag.

Naomi *opens the bag and removes a little cake box.*

Charlie   There's a selection of cakes in there.

Naomi   For me?

Charlie   Yes.

Naomi   Why?

Charlie   I know how much you like my cake.

She gives him a suspicious look.

Charlie   . . . I said some nasty shit to you . . . It's my way of apologising.

Naomi   I don't need an apology. But thanks.

Charlie   You're welcome.

Naomi *puts the cake box on the table.*

Charlie   . . . I miss you.

Naomi   Don't start.

Charlie   I do.

Naomi   No you don't.

Charlie   I think *I* might know how *I'm* feeling –

Naomi   You miss having someone to do your laundry.

Charlie   I miss *you*.

Naomi   I'm not coming back.

Charlie   We could at least talk about it –

Naomi   I am not coming back!

Charlie   Well, let's park that conversation for now.

Beat.

I spoke to your mum.

Naomi   . . . What for?

Charlie   She called me.

Naomi   Right. And . . .?

Charlie   She's worried.

Naomi   About what?

Charlie   You. She said you're not returning her calls.

Naomi   I've been busy.

Charlie   Doing what?

Naomi   Sorry?

Charlie   What are you busy doing?

Naomi   I have a life, Charlie! I have a job! I've a lot on my plate –

Charlie   Okay. Alright. I'm only asking . . . Anyway, I had to tell her you'd moved out.

Naomi   For fuck's sake! Whatcha do that for?

Charlie   I wasn't gonna lie to her, was I?

Naomi   Why not?

Charlie   Because . . .

Naomi   Jesus Christ.

Charlie   Just give her a call.

Naomi   Fine. I will.

Beat.

Charlie   I also spoke to Jada.

Naomi   Oh.

Charlie (*nods*)   . . . You been in touch with her?

Naomi   Obviously, yes . . . We spoke like . . . last week.

Charlie   She's really taking it all very hard.

Naomi   Charlie, I don't need this.

Charlie   I'm concerned about her.

Naomi   Please. You don't give a fuck.

Charlie   Why would you say that?

Naomi   You're loving all this. Another chance for you to play the victim. Paint me as the heartless devil bitch mom –

Charlie   Oh stop –

Naomi   It's true.

Charlie   Where do you get such a warped perception of reality?

Naomi   Will you just leave? Seriously. This is fucking pointless.

Charlie   Alright. Okay. I'll be on my way. No sense having an argument.

Naomi   No. There's not.

Charlie   Agreed. Well. Good to see you. Let's talk again soon.

Naomi (*'I hope not'*)   Mm-hmm.

Charlie (*remembers something*)   Oh! There was one other thing. Do you remember Riley?

Naomi   Who?

Charlie   Jada's mate. Tall bloke. Blond. You must remember him. He's been at the house a couple of times.

Naomi (*non-committal*)   Sure.

Charlie   Yeah, so he came into the tea room yesterday. Told me he'd seen you at the gym.

Naomi (*rising panic*)   . . . Okay . . .?

Charlie   . . . Have you started going?

Naomi   Eh, yes.

Charlie   And . . .? How is it . . .?

Naomi   Fine.

Charlie   Fine . . .? That's all you're gonna say . . .?

Naomi   Yes. It's fine.

Charlie   Okay . . . Well. Good. I'm glad you're doing that. Glad you took my advice.

Naomi *forces a fake smile. Beat.*

Charlie   Alright then. I guess I'll make tracks –

Naomi   I'm seeing someone else.

Charlie   Sorry?

Naomi   I lied to you before. I *am* seeing someone.

Charlie   . . . Oh . . . Who?

Naomi   You don't need to know who.

Charlie   . . . Is it someone from school?

Naomi   No.

Charlie   Is it Kevin?

Naomi (*'don't be ridiculous'*)   No!

Charlie   Who then?

Naomi   No one you know.

Offstage, the main door of the flat opens and shuts. Someone has entered the property.

Charlie   How long?

Naomi   What?

Charlie   How long have you been –?

Naomi   Not long.

Charlie   When did it start? Was it before you moved out?

Naomi   . . . No.

Charlie   I don't believe you.

Naomi   Charlie –

Charlie   You're a liar –

Naomi   Alright! Fine! It started before I moved out! Okay! Are you happy now?

Beat. **Charlie** *opens the cake box. He picks up a piece of cake –*

Naomi   What you doing –?

– and he smooshes it into **Naomi***'s face –*

Naomi   No! Get off! Stop it –

As this is happening, **Kash** *enters –*

Charlie   Fuck you –

Kash   Woah –

Naomi   Jesus –

Kash   What's going on?

Naomi   . . . Nothing . . . Charlie was just leaving.

Beat. **Charlie** *rushes out through the back door.*

Kash   Eh . . . what the fuck was that?

Naomi   Nothing.

Kash   Are you okay?

Naomi   I'm fine. I'm fine. How are you? God. What did the midwife say? Where's Zoe?

Kash   Eh, she's in the bedroom.

Naomi   Is everything alright? What's the story –?

Kash   Hang on. Sorry. Hold on. There's cake all over your face. What the hell just happened?

Naomi Nothing happened . . . We had a disagreement. That's all.

Kash A disagreement?

Naomi Yes.

Kash That seemed like more than a disagreement. He like assaulted you. With a Victoria Sponge –

Naomi It was nothing. Honestly . . . I told him I'm seeing someone else.

Kash Oh . . . Shit.

Naomi Yeah, so he was upset, obviously . . .

Kash Right, so he – Fuck –

Naomi It's fine. It's no big deal. What about you guys? Is the baby okay?

Kash Oh, man . . .

Naomi . . . What? What is it?

Kash . . . Eh, alright, well . . . The hormone levels in Zoe's womb are – they're like messed up.

Naomi Okay?

Kash Yeah, which, apparently, that indicates the baby might have a genetic disorder.

Naomi Right . . .? So . . .?

Kash So . . . (*repeating something he's heard at the hospital*) the foetus may not be viable.

Naomi Oh my God –

Kash Could die in the womb. Could live for a year. Could have Down's Syndrome. Could be fine. We don't know.

Naomi Fuck . . . So – so – what happens now?

Kash   Zoe had to do this like DNA test. Now we just – we gotta wait for the results.

Naomi   Wait how long?

Kash   Eh, they said they'd call within five days.

Naomi   Christ . . . I'm sorry . . . I dunno what to say . . . If there's anything I can do . . .

Kash   Thank you.

Naomi   . . . Zoe must be . . .

Kash   Yeah, she's . . .

He shakes his head, sighs.

Naomi   No, of course . . . Are you alright . . .?

Kash   . . . I dunno . . . I'm a bit . . . I'll be fine. I'm sure everything will . . .

Naomi   Yes!

Kash   Yeah . . . It's just . . . It's not what we – (*Suddenly tearful.*) Shit. Sorry –

Naomi   Oh, hey, come on –

Kash   No, no, I'm okay. I'm alright. Sorry. I just – I been holding it together all afternoon, you know. I didn't want Zoe to . . .

Naomi   Come here.

She hugs him.

Blackout.

Scene Two

The next day. Night-time.

Zoe *sits at the kitchen table in the dark, looking at her phone.* **Naomi** *enters.*

Naomi (*jumps*)   Woah. Jesus. Zoe.

Zoe   Hey.

Naomi   . . . You scared me.

Zoe   Sorry.

Naomi   . . . What you doing?

Zoe (*shrugs*)   . . . Sitting.

Naomi   In the dark . . .?

Zoe   Can't sleep, so . . .

Naomi   Right. Me neither . . .

She gets a glass of water. Beat.

Naomi   Kash told me. The news . . .

Zoe   . . .

Naomi   You wanna talk about / it –?

Zoe   Nope.

Naomi   . . . Might be a good idea –

Zoe   I don't wanna talk, okay. Just leave me alone.

Naomi   . . . No. Alright. Well . . . If you change your mind –

Zoe   Yep.

Naomi   . . . Don't stay up too late . . . Good night.

Zoe   Night.

Naomi *goes to leave – but she stops. Beat.*

Naomi   Come out with me tomorrow night.

Zoe   What?

Naomi   Lemme take you to dinner.

Zoe   I don't wanna go to dinner. I don't wanna go
anywhere.

Naomi   . . . I could use a friend.

Zoe   . . . Are you fucking serious?

Naomi   I know. I'm sorry. I just . . .

Zoe (*sighs*)   . . . What's the matter?

Naomi   Nothing. Never mind –

Zoe   Tell me! What's wrong?

Beat.

Naomi   . . . I told Charlie about Rocco.

Zoe   Oh –

Naomi   So, obviously, he calls Jada. Tells her I cheated on him.

Zoe   What –?

Naomi   She calls me. Tells me I am – and I quote – 'a disgusting, immoral cunt'. Says she never wants to speak to me again.

Zoe   Fuck.

Naomi   Yeah, so . . . I dunno what the hell I'm doing. I feel like I've ruined my whole life just so I could have sex with a man who – what was I thinking? – he's like half my age.

Zoe   . . . You haven't ruined your whole life.

Naomi *shrugs.*

Zoe   Give Jada some time. She'll . . .

Naomi   Yeah, maybe . . . God. It's her birthday at the weekend. I'm supposed to be going up to see her. With Charlie. (*Beat.*) Sorry. I know you don't need this right now –

Zoe   It's fine.

Naomi   Are *you* . . .? How are you?

Zoe   I'm . . . shit.

Naomi No, sure . . . Look, though, I don't think you should just sit around here all week worrying.

Zoe What the hell else am I supposed to do? It's all I can think about.

Naomi No. Obviously, but – I dunno. Go for a walk. Get some exercise.

Zoe I don't wanna see anybody. I don't wanna leave the house.

Naomi Well, okay. Talk to people then, at least. Talk to me. Talk to Kash.

Zoe I can't talk to Kash.

Naomi Why not?

Zoe I just can't.

Naomi . . . He's upset too, you know.

Zoe I know he's upset. That's not . . . (*Beat.*) Can I share something with you?

Naomi Of course.

Zoe You have to promise not to tell him.

Naomi I won't . . . I promise.

Zoe . . . This isn't my first pregnancy.

Naomi . . .?

Zoe I had an abortion when I was nineteen.

Naomi Oh. Okay. And Kash doesn't know –?

Zoe No, and you can't tell him. Seriously. I need you to promise –

Naomi I'm not gonna say anything. I promise.

Zoe Thank you.

Naomi . . . So . . .?

Zoe   So, yeah, so that's like – I dunno – that's in my head now. Because . . . you know it took us ages to conceive, right?

Naomi   Eh, yeah –

Zoe   It took us like a year almost, and the whole time I just – I felt like – I felt like I was being punished.

Naomi   Oh come on –

Zoe   No, for real. I felt like God, or the universe, or whatever, was punishing me. For what I'd done. The first time.

Naomi   That's not –

Zoe   That's how I felt.

Naomi   Jesus –

Zoe   But then . . . it happened, right? I got pregnant. And it was – I mean, I was nauseous and I was worried about the baby and money and all sorts of other shit – but none of that really mattered. I was – I wasn't just *happy* – For the first time in my life, it felt like everything had fallen into place, you know. I was doing what I was meant to do. I felt fucking *whole*. And maybe more than anything I felt grateful. For another chance . . . Then the phone call comes from the midwife. And now here I am. It just feels like I'm being punished all over again –

Naomi   You're not being punished.

Zoe   I dunno how else to see it.

Naomi   Listen, I don't mean to be insensitive, but I think you're twisting this into something much worse than it actually is.

Zoe   How could it be any worse?

Naomi   Because. This kinda thing happens all the time. Prob'ly every day there are women in the same situation as you. And ninety-nine per cent of the time, it's fine. *You*'ll be fine. Before you know it, you'll be screaming at the doctor for an emergency C-section.

Zoe   Gee, thanks.

Naomi   Parenting is shit, alright! It is! It's shit! It's not joy.
Or fulfilment. It doesn't fucking make you whole, pet! Sorry!
It's – It's a tsunami of guilt and anxiety and exhaustion.
What you're going through now – it's only the beginning.

Zoe (*gentle sarcasm*)   Okay, great.

Naomi   It's true. You know what, full disclosure – don't
judge me, but I used to fantasise about murdering my own
baby.

Zoe   What?

Naomi   I wasn't actually gonna do it. It was just – I had
these thoughts. These like intrusive thoughts. That I'd . . .
indulge in sometimes.

Zoe   What kinda thoughts?

Naomi   I dunno. Like we'd be out walking when she was
really small: I'd get this urge to like let go of the pushchair.
Watch it roll gloriously down the hill into the onrushing
traffic.

Zoe   Jesus –

Naomi   Or I'd be feeding her at like three in the morning.
Suddenly I'd get this image in my mind: I'm smashing her
tiny body against the wall. Lady Macbeth style.

Zoe   Fucking hell –

Naomi   This is the journey you are on now, you know.
Welcome to motherhood, bitch!

Zoe   . . . I think you've actually made me feel worse. If
that's possible.

Naomi   Ah, fuck off. (*Beat.*) Come on. Whadiya say? Dinner.
Tomorrow night.

Zoe   I don't wanna go to dinner.

Naomi   So, what? You're just gonna lock yourself away for the whole half-term break?

Zoe   Until the phone call comes, yes.

Naomi   Fuck that. I'm taking you out.

Zoe   I don't wanna go out.

Naomi   I don't wanna fucking go either, if you're gonna be this miserable about it. But that's what's happening.

Zoe   God almighty . . . Let me see how I feel tomorrow. Alright?

Naomi   . . . Alright. Fine . . . Go to bed now, will you?

Zoe   I think I fucking will actually. Get away from you.

Naomi   Good! Good night.

Zoe   Good night.

Naomi (*calls as* **Zoe** *goes*)   And talk to your husband!

Zoe *is gone.*

Zoe (*offstage*)   Yeah, yeah.

Naomi (*to herself*)   Or you'll end up like me.

Blackout.

Scene Three

The next day. Morning.

Kash, *barefoot, in his dressing gown, prepares breakfast, consulting a recipe on his phone –*

Kash   Right, let's see . . . (*Consults his phone.*) Flour . . .

He opens a cupboard.

(*Surprise.*) The airlock is open, captain . . .

He looks inside.

(*Fear.*) The airlock is open, captain . . .

He removes a bag of flour and puts it down on one of the kitchen surfaces.

(*Consults his phone.*) Sugar . . .

He looks in the cupboard again . . .

(*Shock.*) . . . What the . . .?! The infrared monitor! There's someone else on board! (*With more panic.*) The infrared monitor! There's someone else on board!

He takes a bag of sugar and places it next to the flour.

(*Consults his phone.*) Eggs. (*Already knows where they are.*) Okay . . .

He places the eggs with the other ingredients.

No, captain. I'm telling you. There is another life form on the ship. (*Consults his phone.*) . . . Buttermilk . . . Fuck.

He opens the fridge. He looks inside.

Captain, you can't ask me to do that!

He takes out a carton of milk, looks at it, shrugs and adds it to the hoard of ingredients.

Naomi *enters.*

Kash (*firmer*)   Captain, you can't ask me to do that!

Naomi   Eh, Kash –?

Kash   Oh. Hey. Sorry. Big audition today. Just running lines.

Naomi   Oh. Right. Eh, I'm heading out.

Kash   Okay.

Naomi   Could you just remind Zoe about our dinner date this evening?

Kash   Eh, sure.

Naomi   I'll text her anyway, but –

Kash   I'll tell her.

Naomi   Thank you.

Kash   No worries . . . Did you speak to her last night?

Naomi   Eh, yeah.

Kash   She seem alright?

Naomi   She'll be fine.

Kash   She's not really talking to me.

Naomi   Don't worry. Honestly . . . How you holding up?

Kash   Ah, you know.

Naomi   You'll be okay.

Kash   Thanks, yeah . . .

Naomi   . . . Well, I better get to the gym –

Kash   Hey, eh, I wanted to say, I'm glad you're here.

Naomi   . . .?

Kash   Not like – I'm not glad your marriage broke down or anything. Just. It's been nice having you with us.

Naomi   Oh. Wow. Kash, that really means a lot. Thank you.

Kash   It's cool.

Naomi   . . . Are you making breakfast?!

Kash   Why do you sound so surprised?

Naomi   No reason.

Kash   I can cook.

Naomi (*'can you?'*)   Uh-huh.

Kash   I am a culinary master.

Naomi   I'll see you later.

Kash   Alright. Have fun.

Naomi   Good luck with the . . .

Kash   Thanks. Bye.

Naomi *exits. Shortly after, we hear her leaving the flat.*

Kash   Okay. Where were we . . .? (*Consults his phone.*) Bicarbonate of soda. Come on. What the fuck?

He looks in the cupboard.

Captain, you can't ask me to do that!

He deliberates for a moment. Then he picks up his phone and makes a call. After a few seconds –

Kash (*into the phone*)   Hey, do we have any bicarbonate of soda . . .? I'm in the kitchen . . . Because I can't be arsed going all the way to the bedroom . . . Bicarbonate of soda . . . No, just tell me where it is . . . Which cupboard . . .? Hello . . .? Zoe . . .?

Zoe *enters, barefoot, in a sleep t-shirt.*

Zoe (*cross*)   What you doing?

Kash   No! You're not allowed in here –

Zoe   Are you making breakfast?

Kash   Can you leave please?

Zoe   What about the bicarbonate of soda?

Kash   . . . Fine. Show me where it is. Then kindly –

Zoe   It's not pancakes, is it? Cos you don't need bicarbonate of soda for pancakes –

Kash   Can you just tell me where it is? And then (*instead of something harsher*) go away –

Zoe *goes to the cupboard.*

Zoe   It's right in front of you.

She hands **Kash** *the bicarbonate of soda. He puts it with the other ingredients –*

Kash   Thank you. (*Pointing her towards the door.*) Now . . .

Zoe   I'm going. I'm going.

She goes to exit – but she stops. Beat.

Zoe   Did Naomi go out?

Kash   Yes.

Zoe (*sighs*)   . . . Maybe we should talk?

Kash   You're ruining my surprise!

Zoe   You called me!

Kash (*exasperation*)   Dah!

Zoe   You don't need to make me breakfast anyway.

Kash   I'm trying do something nice for you.

Zoe   That's kind of you. Thanks. You're very sweet.

Kash   . . . Fine. You can stay.

Zoe   Okay.

Kash   Sit down. I'll make you some tea.

Zoe   It's alright. I'll get myself some water.

Kash   Okay. Sure. You just – You gotta let me concentrate on the –

Zoe   Yes, chef.

Kash (*a fake laugh*)   Ha-ha. (*Remembers.*) Oh, eh, Naomi said she's still on for dinner this evening.

Zoe (*groans*)   Ugh. Okay.

Kash   You should go.

Zoe   Yeah, maybe. I dunno.

Kash You and me could do something this afternoon. After my audition.

Zoe I think I just wanna stay home.

Kash Come on. Let's go out.

Zoe Don't you have work?

Kash Eh, no.

Zoe Why not?

Kash . . . I kinda lost my job.

Zoe What?!

Kash Obviously I went to the hospital. I missed my shift. Alberto was a total dick about it.

Zoe He fired you?

Kash Words were exchanged.

Zoe You resigned?

Kash He was gonna sack me anyway.

Zoe For fuck's sake! When were you gonna tell me this?

Kash I didn't wanna worry you . . . Look, let's be positive here. It means I'm free this afternoon. We can catch a movie together.

Zoe I don't wanna catch a movie. I want you to go find another fucking job.

Kash I will. I've got the Netflix thing this morning. We're talking big money.

Zoe *If* you get it. *If* –

Kash Which I really think I will! Seriously. I've got such a good feeling about this one.

Zoe Yeah, you always have a good feeling.

Kash What's that supposed to mean?

Zoe   Nothing. Just . . . Go do your audition. Whatever. You're such an asshole sometimes!

Kash   I think you're the asshole here!

Zoe   I thought it was the hospital just now!

Kash   Huh?

Zoe   When you called. To ask about the fucking bicarbonate of soda. I thought the hospital was –

Kash   Oh shit.

Zoe   . . . It's okay. I just got a fright.

Kash   I'm sorry. I guess I *am* an asshole.

Zoe   No, you're not . . . You're an awesome human being. And I love you.

Kash   I love you too. (*A joke.*) Most of the time.

Zoe   Shut up.

Kash   . . . Maybe they *will* call today.

Zoe   Maybe.

Beat.

Hey, I'm sorry I've been a bit . . . distant.

Kash   That's okay.

Zoe   I guess I've just been trying to process everything.

Kash   No, of course. You don't need to explain . . . How are you feeling like physically?

Zoe   Alright, I guess. Apart from the nausea, and the back pain, and the constipation –

Kash   Oh –

Zoe   The usual shit. Which I can cope with. It's just the anxiety. Jesus –

Kash (*agreement*)   No –

Zoe   And I'm angry, you know, as well.

Kash   Absolutely.

Zoe   I'm angry with *you*.

Kash   . . . Why are you angry with me –?

Zoe   Because. I'm fucked off this is happening to *my* body. Not yours.

Kash   . . . What is? The pregnancy?

Zoe   The pregnancy. The Harmony Test. All of it.

Kash   Right. I mean, you know men can't –

Zoe   I know you can't carry a fucking child! I know that! I can still be cross about it!

Kash   Okay.

Zoe   Sorry.

Kash   No . . .

Zoe   I'm cross with myself too.

Kash   Because . . .?

Zoe   . . . This is gonna sound stupid, but I spent a lot of time, you know, before the scan, like visualising the baby and almost like getting to know her and like accepting her into my body, and then the call came and it was like suddenly the child I imagined – (*Suddenly tearful.*) she was gone –

Kash (*holds her hand*)   Hey –

Zoe   Like I lost her. And that just – I've started to feel like the baby's not a baby anymore . . . Like it's not even human. It's a monster . . . And now part of me just wants to get rid of it. Just get it out of my body. And that makes me feel angry and like guilty and just fucking . . .

Kash   Hey. It's alright.

For a moment, they hold hands without speaking. Beat.

Zoe   How would you feel – if we had to . . .?

Kash   Like . . .?

Zoe   An abortion.

Beat. **Kash** *lets go of* **Zoe**'s *hand.*

Kash   . . . It's not what I want.

Zoe   No, obviously. It's not what I want either, but like, if the result is . . .

Kash   Yeah –

Zoe   I don't know if I could cope, you know, if the child is like severely disabled, or it's only gonna live for like a few months anyway . . .

Kash   . . . Honestly . . . I think my instinct – this is our child – whether it's healthy or 'normal' or whatever – it's our child – we should love and accept it.

Zoe   Of course, yes. I *want* to love it. I do. But like . . . we gotta be practical here. Who's actually gonna look after it?

Kash   We are –

Zoe   Let's say it's bedbound. Needs twenty-four-hour care. Can't move. Can't talk. Can't feed itself. Can't control its own bowel movements. Just lies there all day. In its own shit. On a fucking drip or something . . . How's that gonna work . . .?

Kash   . . . I'm not sure –

Zoe   And what do our lives look like . . .? What freedom do we have . . .? I dunno, maybe you're expecting *me* to just –

Kash   No –

Zoe   While you're off shooting for Netflix or whatever –

Kash   What? No. That's not fair –

Zoe That's what happens though, isn't it . . .? It always falls on the woman . . . Sorry, but I don't think I could do that. I don't think I'd *want* to do that.

Kash   . . . We could hire help.

Zoe With what money . . .? Seriously . . .? Where's the money coming from . . .?

Kash We'd figure something out.

Zoe How . . .? *Are* you actually gonna give up acting? Are you . . .? You gonna go work in a fucking bank or something . . .?

Kash   . . . No –

Zoe Well, what then . . .?

Kash   . . . I dunno . . . So what're you saying? You just – you don't wanna have the baby? If there's any kinda problem or like abnormality, that's it. It's over –

Zoe No –

Kash Unless it's like a perfect genetic specimen –

Zoe No! I dunno what I'm saying! I dunno what I'm saying . . . I *do* wanna have the baby. You fucking know that . . . I just . . . I dunno what I want . . . I dunno what's best . . . I'm completely fucking . . .

Beat.

Kash Listen, I get that this is – it's shit. It's so shit. For you, in particular. It's fucking horrible. I'm just saying, you know, after everything we've been through to get this far, it seems crazy to even think about –

Zoe Jesus Christ . . .

Kash   . . . But, okay, fine, yeah, practically . . . maybe, it's not . . . I dunno . . . (*Beat.*) Ultimately, whatever you choose, I will support your decision.

Zoe   . . . *My* decision?

Kash   It's your body so . . .

Zoe   So it's my responsibility?

Kash   No, not just you –

Zoe   You don't think we should come to a decision together? The two of us?

Kash   Yes, of course, but . . . Look, let's just wait until we get the result. And then we can . . .

Beat. **Zoe** *gets up.*

Kash   What you doing?

Zoe   I'm going back to bed.

Kash   Eh, okay. Shall I bring the breakfast in?

Zoe   I'm not hungry.

Kash   But like –

Zoe   I wanna be alone please –

Kash   Zoe –

Zoe   I hope the audition goes well.

She exits.

Kash   Come on . . .

Beat. **Kash** *picks up the carton of eggs and smashes it into the sink –*

Kash   Fuck.

Blackout.

Scene Four

Later that day.

Kash *and* **Charlie** *are in the kitchen, drunk. There's a mess of empty beer bottles and cans, maybe a bottle of whiskey, on the table.*

Charlie   . . . So the thing with the cake . . . I'm sorry you had to see that . . . I felt upset, you know . . . Betrayed . . .

Kash *gives* **Charlie**'s *shoulder a comforting pat. Beat.*

Charlie   Men have it tough.

Kash   I know.

Charlie   Women are cruel.

Kash   Yes.

Charlie   And like mean.

Kash   They're very mean.

Charlie   And hurtful. They are cruel, mean, hurtful creatures.

Kash   True dat, brother.

They drink. Beat.

Charlie   I'm not saying women have it easy.

Kash   No.

Charlie   . . . Childbirth, for example.

Kash   Yes –

Charlie   By all accounts, childbirth is quite hard.

Kash   Quite, yeah.

Charlie   . . . And there's menstruation.

Kash   Yes.

Charlie   It's every month, you know.

Kash   I know.

Charlie   . . . And then like the menopause.

Kash   The menopause.

Charlie   That's *real*.

Kash   It is.

Charlie   And, of course, thousands of years of patriarchal oppression.

Kash   Patriarchy, yeah. Not good.

Charlie   Women have a lot to contend with.

Kash   Certainly, yes.

Charlie   Still though. Men have it tough.

Kash   We do. We really do.

Beat.

Charlie   My wife hates me.

Kash   Same.

Charlie   Really?

Kash   Yep.

Charlie   You and Zoe . . .?

Kash   Pfff.

Charlie   I thought you two –?

Kash   She won't even talk to me.

Charlie   Fuck.

Kash   I know.

Charlie   Give you some advice . . .

Kash   Sure.

Charlie   Keep working at it.

Kash   Yeah –?

Charlie   Treat it like a job, you know.

Kash   Okay.

Charlie   It *is* a job.

Kash   It is?

Charlie   It's your main job. Your marriage is your main job.

Kash   Right.

Charlie   You gotta work at it.

Kash   Sure –

Charlie   Don't let it drift. A woman needs attention. Twenty-four hours a day. *Twenty-four*. Don't sleep. You think you can sleep. You can't fucking sleep. You gotta be on it. All the time. Restaurants. Flowers. Housework. All of that shit. You need computers! And like spreadsheets. You need staff. You need a team of staff. Otherwise . . . Forget it. You're fucked.

Kash   No, I hear ya.

Offstage, the main door of the flat opens and shuts. Someone has entered the property.

Charlie   Thing is, right. It's not too late for you.

Kash   No.

Charlie   You can still –

Kash   I know.

Charlie   Me, though –

Kash   Come on.

Charlie   I'm done.

Kash   No?

Charlie   We're finished.

Kash   I'm sorry, man.

Beat.

Charlie   She cheated on me.

Kash   Yeah?

Charlie   She told me.

Kash   Oh.

Charlie   So . . .

Kash   Fuck, man.

Charlie   It's over.

Rocco *stumbles into the kitchen – he's drunk too.*

Rocco   Whoops a daisy . . .

Kash (*sudden panic*)   . . . Rocco . . .

Rocco   Oh! Hi, guys!

Charlie   Hey, man –

Rocco   Hey –

Kash   What's going on?

Rocco   No, nothing, nothing. Been out, you know. Feeling a bit . . . Beer. Wine. Vodka Red Bull . . .

Kash   Right –

Rocco   Sorry to barge in on you –

Charlie   Don't be silly –

Rocco (*re the empty bottles*)   Are you having a party?

Kash   / No –

Charlie   Yes, we are –

Kash   Few beverages. That's all –

Charlie   You want one?

Rocco   God, I shouldn't –

Kash   I don't think we have any left actually –

Charlie   Course we do. Go on, mate.

Rocco   Nah. Honestly. I been at it since lunchtime –

Kash You take a break. Sleep it off –

Charlie Have a beer with us!

Rocco . . . Alright! Fuck it!

Charlie Good man!

He gives **Rocco** *a beer.*

Charlie Who are you?

Rocco I don't even know.

Charlie Me neither, buddy. Me neither. Cheers.

Kash (*'what do I do?'*) Cheers –

Rocco Cheers!

Throughout the following, **Kash** *gestures silently to* **Rocco** *in an attempt to alert him to the peril he faces –* **Rocco** *fails to read the signals.*

Rocco So what's happening?

Kash Not much. Just chatting, you know –

Charlie I'd say we were on an exploratory journey through the quagmire of twenty-first-century gender relations.

Rocco Oh. Okay . . . Fancy a sing-song?

Kash Eh, no, not really our vibe –

Charlie That is a fucking great idea!

Rocco Yes, bruv!

Charlie What shall we sing?

Kash I'm on voice rest actually –

Rocco How do you feel about Shania Twain?

Kash Nooo –

Charlie I fucking love Shania Twain!

Rocco   Really?

Kash   Really?

Charlie   What song?

Rocco   . . . 'You're Still the One'?

Kash   That is a / terrible song –

Charlie   Oh my God, that's basically my favourite song of all time.

Rocco   Me too!

Charlie   Ready, lads?

Kash   / Nah –

Charlie *and* **Rocco** *start to sing 'You're Still the One'.* **Charlie** *throws his arm around* **Rocco**'s *shoulder.* **Kash** *resists, but soon –*

Kash   Fuck it.

He joins the singing. After the first chorus, they break off –

Rocco   Jesus, I need a break, lads.

Charlie   No, come on. Don't stop.

Rocco   Nah, seriously, man. I'm totally fucked. I need to go lie down.

Kash (*trying to get* **Rocco** *out of the room*)   Yeah, why don't you eh –?

Rocco   Is Naomi in?

Beat.

Kash   . . . No. She's eh – she's out to dinner. With Zoe.

Rocco   Oh, okay. I might just . . .

Charlie   Sorry, who did you say you were?

Kash   Ehm –

Rocco   I'm Rocco.

Charlie   Rocco?

Kash   Charlie, this is Rocco. Rocco: Charlie.

Rocco   Charlie?

Kash   Yes.

Rocco   Oh –

Charlie   How do you know Naomi?

Rocco   . . . Who, sorry?

Charlie   Naomi . . .?

Rocco   . . . I don't.

Charlie   You just asked if she was here.

Rocco   Did I?

Charlie   Yes.

Rocco   Oh, no, yeah. We're, eh – we're gym buddies.

Charlie   Gym buddies?

Rocco   / Yes –

Kash   Anyway, 'bout time we wrapped it up, / I think –

Charlie   What does that mean? Why are you in Kash's house? (*To* **Kash**.) Why is he in your house?

Rocco   You know what – I just remembered something. I gotta –

Charlie   No, hold on. Wait . . . Are you . . .? (*To* **Kash**.) Is he . . .? Is this the guy . . .? Is he the . . .?

Kash   . . . I, eh –

Charlie   Yes or no? Is it him?

Kash   Yes –

Rocco   Oh fuck –

Charlie   This guy . . .?

Kash *nods.*

Charlie   But . . . but he's like – he's a twelve-year-old!

Kash   I'm pretty sure he's in twenties.

Rocco   I'm twenty-five next month –

Charlie   Oh my God, this is like – (*Hyper-ventilating.*) This is very triggering for me!

Kash   Well, sure –

Rocco   Sorry, mate –

Charlie   Why didn't you tell me who he was?

Kash   How am I supposed to tell you? He's standing in the room with us –

Rocco   It woulda been awkward.

Charlie   It *is* awkward! He let me sing a song with you!

Kash   I tried to stop you! I fucking hate Shania Twain –

Charlie   Jesus –

Rocco   I'm really sorry –

Charlie (*to* **Kash**)   What the fuck is wrong with you?

Kash   It's not my fault! It's him you should be angry with!

Rocco   He's right –

Charlie   Fucking asshole!

He pushes **Kash**.

Kash   Hey. Whatcha do that for?

Charlie   You deserve it!

Rocco   No, come on –

Charlie *pushes* **Kash** *again.*

Kash   Stop it.

Charlie   No –

Another push.

Rocco   Guys –

Kash   Stop pushing me.

Another push.

Rocco   Stop –

Kash   I'll push you back, man.

He pushes **Charlie**.

Charlie   Whadiya pushing me for?

Kash   You pushed me first!

Rocco   / Seriously –

Charlie   Right, that's it!

He grabs **Kash**, *and suddenly they're grappling with one another.*

Rocco   No. Stop it . . . Fuck . . .

He tries to intervene – and now we have a three-way struggle: a messy, inelegant scrum, more pathetic than violent, during which the actors ad-lib – 'Let go!', 'Get off!', 'You get off!', 'Watch my hair, man!', 'You're hurting my finger!', etc. As the fight unfolds, offstage, we hear the front door of the flat open and close. Shortly after, **Zoe** *and* **Naomi** *enter. They watch in stunned silence. Eventually, the tussle ends with all three men lying on the kitchen floor, panting. After a silence . . .*

Zoe   What? The actual? Fuck . . .?

Rocco   Ladies –

Charlie   Oh, look who it is –

Zoe   What is going on?

Kash   . . .

Naomi   What are you . . .?! Why are you . . .?! What . . .?!

Charlie   Look, don't you start. This is all your fault.

Naomi   . . . Excuse me?

Charlie (*clambers to his feet*)   Lemme tell you something, yeah. Lemme just tell you something . . . Nineteen years, we were married, okay. *Nineteen* years. And, you know, in many ways, I was happy –

Naomi   What's / happening –?

Charlie   Nice house. Wonderful daughter –

Naomi   / What's he doing –?

Charlie   The whole fucking fairy tale, right. *But* – the truth is, in all that time, not a day went by – not a single day in nineteen years when I didn't feel a very powerful urge to fuck another woman.

Naomi   Oh dear God –

Kash   Charlie, mate –

Charlie   No, don't fucking – No! She might not wanna hear it, but it's the truth! To be a man, yeah – To be a man, it's not just to be preoccupied, or, or, or, obsessed even, with sex – to be a man is to be physically primed for sex at all times. Like a gun waiting to go off –

Naomi   Jesus –

Kash   You don't need to do this –

Charlie   It's the fucking truth! The sun shines. The wind blows. Men wanna fuck!

Naomi   Stop –

Charlie   A woman comes into the tea room. My mind, my body, my instinct, everything tells me to fuck her –

Naomi   / Enough –

Charlie   There's a woman at the bus stop: fuck her. The woman on the telly: fuck her. The woman at the funeral: fuck her –

Naomi   / Please –

Charlie   I'm walking down the street: fuck her. Fuck her. Fuck her. Fuck her. I wanna fuck all of them. All of the time. Everywhere I go. For *nineteen* years. *Now* . . . how many of those women do I actually fuck . . .? How many, Naomi . . .?

Naomi   Somebody make/ him stop –

Kash   / Come on –

Charlie   None! Not a single one. I never cheated on you. Not once. *Not once*. Okay, I watched a little porn –

Naomi   / Aw –

Charlie   Fine: a lot of porn. The internet is a fucking curse. But I never cheated on you. Never even came close –

Naomi   / Stop it –

Charlie   Which. Come on. Can you imagine the strength that took? The character? Every cell in my body is *on fire*. I am *burning*. I just wanna fuck. *All* of me wants to do it, and it's *all* I wanna do – always. But I don't. I don't do it. *I do not fuck*. No! Not even once do I give in. And do you know why?

Naomi   . . .

Charlie   Because I made a vow to my wife. I made a vow to you, Naomi. And, to me, that means something. That vow – that vow is important, yeah . . . Can you not see . . .? Can you not understand . . .? Nineteen years, I deny myself. Boom. You fuck someone else. How is that fair? How? How could you do that? You just – You just replace me. The man you raised a child with. You replace. With, with this guy. Who, he's the same fucking age as our daughter. I mean, what is that?

Naomi   Go home, Charlie, please.

Charlie   That's it, is it? That's all you got? 'Go home'.

Naomi   Go on. Go. Leave.

Charlie   Fuck you! Fuck all of ya!

He exits via the back door. Beat.

Kash   So, how was Pizza Express?

Zoe *shakes her head and exits.*

Naomi   Come talk to me in the bedroom.

Rocco   I might head home as well actually . . . Not feeling very talkative . . . (*Off* **Naomi***'s look.*) Okay, I'm coming. (*To* **Kash**.) See ya, mate.

Naomi *and* **Rocco** *exit. Beat.* **Kash** *begins to tidy away the bottles and cans.*

Blackout.

Scene Five

The next morning.

Zoe *sits alone at the kitchen table, looking at her phone. On the table, there's a box of cornflakes. After a few moments, she puts the phone aside abruptly. She looks around – she wants to get rid of it. She makes a decision – she puts the phone into the box of cornflakes. She sits back in her seat and tries to regulate her breathing.*

Kash *enters, dishevelled and hungover.*

Kash   Anything . . .?

Zoe   No.

Kash *sighs in frustration. He guzzles some water, perhaps straight from the tap.*

Kash   Fucking hell, my head . . . I think I need another beer . . . (*Off her look.*) That was a joke.

Zoe *is not impressed.*

Kash   Look, I know you're cross with me . . . I didn't plan to . . . Charlie just turned up and like . . . You know I don't get drunk. I don't do that . . . I'm sorry . . . It won't happen again . . .

Zoe   It's fine.

Kash   . . . Are you okay?

Zoe *shrugs.*

Kash   . . . You're not gonna talk to me?

Zoe   What do you want me to say?

Kash   I dunno. Anything . . . Maybe we should talk through some of the like scenarios, or options, or whatever.

Zoe   You said you wanted to wait 'til we get the result.

Kash   No, I know, but . . . fine . . . I just wish they'd fucking call, you know . . . It's like – If we don't find out today, we're gonna have to stew on it all weekend, which . . . how is that right . . .?

Beat.

You got your phone on you?

Zoe   It's here.

Kash   . . . Where?

Zoe   It's in the cornflakes.

Kash   Huh?

Zoe   I put it in the . . . .

Kash   In the box . . .?

Zoe   Yeah.

Kash   . . . Whatcha do that for?

Zoe   I'm sick of waiting for it to ring. I'm sick of looking at it.

Kash   Eh, okay . . . Maybe we should take it out though?

Zoe   I don't wanna take it out.

Kash   What if they call?

Zoe   We'll hear it. It's not on 'Silent'.

Kash   Sure, but . . . Come on. Can we just take it out please?

Zoe   No.

Kash   But like –

Zoe   I don't wanna take it out, okay!

Kash   . . . Okay.

A knock on the back door.

Kash   What now?

Kash *opens the door.*

Charlie (*offstage, in the doorway*)   Hey.

Kash (*'what are you doing here?'*)   Alright.

Charlie   Can I talk to Naomi?

Kash   Eh –

Charlie   She's expecting me.

Kash   Oh. Sure. Come in.

Charlie *enters.*

Kash   I'll eh . . .

Charlie *nods.* **Kash** *exits to the hallway.*

Charlie   Alright.

Zoe *forces a polite smile. A moment of awkwardness before –*

Charlie   It's Jada's birthday. We're going up to visit her.

Zoe   Oh . . .

Another awkward moment.

Charlie   Look. I'm sorry about the . . . Bit too much to drink . . .

Zoe *nods.* **Naomi** *enters, followed by* **Kash**.

Naomi   Yes . . .?

Charlie   You ready?

Naomi   I'm getting the train.

Charlie   We agreed we'd drive up together.

Naomi   I'm not getting in a car with you.

Charlie   Why not?

Naomi   I don't wanna be anywhere near you.

Charlie   For fuck's sake . . . Can we talk outside a minute please?

Naomi   Worried you might embarrass yourself, are you?

Kash   Eh, we can –

Naomi   No. Stay where you are. It's your house.

Charlie   Jesus Christ . . . I'm sorry, okay . . .

Naomi (*'not good enough'*)   . . .

Beat.

Charlie   . . . I need you to drive.

Naomi   What?

Charlie   I'm hungover. I'm a mess. I can't drive all the way to York.

Naomi   Not my problem.

Charlie   Please . . . We can't go up separately.

Naomi   Sure we can.

Charlie   Jada is expecting us to be together. To be a family.

Naomi   Fuck off.

Charlie   It's her birthday.

Naomi   I know it's her fucking birthday! I know that! I gave birth to her!

Beat.

Did you get a present?

Charlie   Huh?

Naomi   Did you get your daughter a birthday present?

Charlie   . . . No.

Naomi *shakes her head.*

Charlie   . . . Did you?

Naomi   Yes! Obviously . . .

Charlie   Fuck.

Beat.

Naomi   . . . We can say it's from the two of us.

Charlie   Thank you.

Naomi   . . . Wait in the car. I'll be there in a minute.

Charlie *exits via the back door. Beat.*

Naomi   Yeah, I've gotta . . .

Zoe *nods.*

Naomi   Any word from –?

Zoe   No.

Naomi   God. (*Beat.*) Well, I should be back on Sunday evening.

Zoe   Fine.

Naomi   . . . Listen, eh, Rocco might drop in at some point over the weekend. Collect some stuff.

Zoe   Okay . . .

Naomi   He left last night.

Kash   Oh –

Naomi   We, eh – we kinda finished.

Kash   You . . .?

Zoe   You broke up?

Naomi   Yes.

Kash   What –?

Zoe   Are you okay?

Naomi   I'm fine.

Kash   Why?

Naomi   . . . He said he wanted some fun. But last night the fun stopped.

Kash   Fuck –

Zoe   Sorry, love –

Naomi   It was my decision. Totally my decision. He's way too young for me.

Kash   Oh. Okay. Still though –

Zoe   That's –

Naomi   Guys, come on – honestly – I'm okay. I'm fine – I need some serious fucking therapy, but apart from that . . . (*Beat.*) Look, I better get going . . .

Zoe   Eh, right –

Naomi   Let me know, please, if you hear anything.

Kash   We will.

Naomi (*to* **Zoe**)   I love you.

Zoe   I love you too.

Naomi *and* **Zoe** *hug.*

Naomi   You're gonna be okay.

When the hug breaks off –

Naomi (*to* **Kash**)   Come here.

Naomi *and* **Kash** *hug.*

Naomi   Look after her, alright?

Kash *nods.*

Naomi   Alright. Bye, guys.

Zoe   Bye.

Kash   See ya.

Naomi *exits to the hallway. Shortly after, we hear her leave the flat. Beat.*

Kash   Wow.

Zoe   I know.

Beat.

Kash   I guess I'll go grab a shower then.

Zoe   Alright.

Kash   I gotta make a fucking self-tape.

Zoe (*gentle sarcasm*)   Oh, good.

Kash   Uh-huh.

Zoe   . . . Hey, how was the Netflix thing?

Kash   It was . . . not bad, I think.

Zoe   Yeah . . .?

Kash   Yeah. I did alright.

Zoe   Great.

Beat.

Kash   Can I do anything for you?

Zoe   No. Thanks.

Kash   Make you some tea?

Zoe *shakes her head.*

Kash   Few pancakes maybe?

Zoe *smiles in spite of herself.*

Kash   You smiled!

Zoe   Fuck off.

Kash   I saw it. I caught you –

Zoe   Go away!

Kash   Alright, alright, I'll eh . . .

Beat.

Zoe   Kash, I'm sorry.

Kash   . . . You've nothing to be sorry for.

Zoe   Yes, I do . . . I'm not like purposely trying to shut you out, or like give you the silent treatment or whatever – I'm just – (*Tearful.*) This whole situation – I can't –

Kash   Hey, it's okay –

Zoe   I just want it to be over.

Kash   Me too . . .

They hug.

Kash   You know I wasn't suggesting you make the decision on your own.

Zoe   No. I know. I'm sorry.

Kash   I'm sorry too.

Zoe   . . . You want me to read with you? (*Off his look.*) For the tape?

Kash   Oh. Really?

Zoe   Sure.

Kash   Eh. Okay. Thanks.

Zoe   Go get your shower.

Kash (*nods*)   . . . Shout, if . . .

Zoe   Yeah.

Kash   Alright.

He is about to exit when the phone rings inside the box of cornflakes. He stops. They look at each other. Beat.

Zoe   Should I –?

Kash   Yes. Quick.

Zoe *removes the phone from the box of cornflakes.*

Zoe (*looks at the phone*)   It's the hospital.

Kash   Okay . . .

She watches it ring.

Kash   Are you gonna . . .?

Zoe   I don't think I can.

Kash   What . . .? Here, give it to me.

Zoe   I don't want to.

Kash   What are you talking about?

Zoe   I don't wanna know.

Kash   Zoe, gimme the phone!

Zoe   No –

Kash (*makes a grab for it*)   Gimme the fucking phone –

Zoe   Stop it!

She drops the phone. It stops ringing.

Kash   Oh my God!

Zoe   I'm sorry. I can't . . .

Kash   We have to get the result! We can't just not . . . Look,
lemme . . . I'm gonna call them back –

She picks up the phone.

Kash   Come on. Please. We need to know.

Zoe   I need you to do it.

Kash   Huh?

Zoe   I can't – I can't listen. I can't be in the room. I'm sorry.

Kash   Alright, that's – I'll do it. I can do it.

She hands him the phone.

Kash (*gestures to the door*)   You want me to . . .?

She nods.

Kash   Okay. Just unlock it for me.

She unlocks the phone.

Kash   I'll be back in a minute.

He exits. **Zoe** *breathes, struggling to contain her emotion. Beat. She
snaps and unleashes her rage on the box of cornflakes. She grabs it,
smashes it, hits it, kicks it, hurls it across the kitchen, stamps on it, the
actor ad-libbing screams, cries, 'Fuck! Fuck you!', etc. Finally, with
the box destroyed and cornflakes strewn everywhere,* **Zoe** *slumps to*

the floor, curls her body into a ball, breathing heavily, trembling, her eyes full of tears. Beat.

Kash *returns. He's tearful too.*

Kash   Zo . . .

She lifts her head. They look at each other. Beat.

Zoe   . . . What is it? Are we gonna be okay?

He goes to her. He gathers her in his arms.

Kash   We're gonna be okay . . . We're gonna be okay . . . We're gonna be okay . . .

They stay together on the floor.

Lights fade.

End of play.

For a complete listing of
Methuen Drama titles, visit:
www.bloomsbury.com/drama

Follow us on Twitter and keep up to date
with our news and publications
@MethuenDrama